I0713677

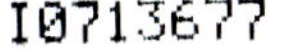

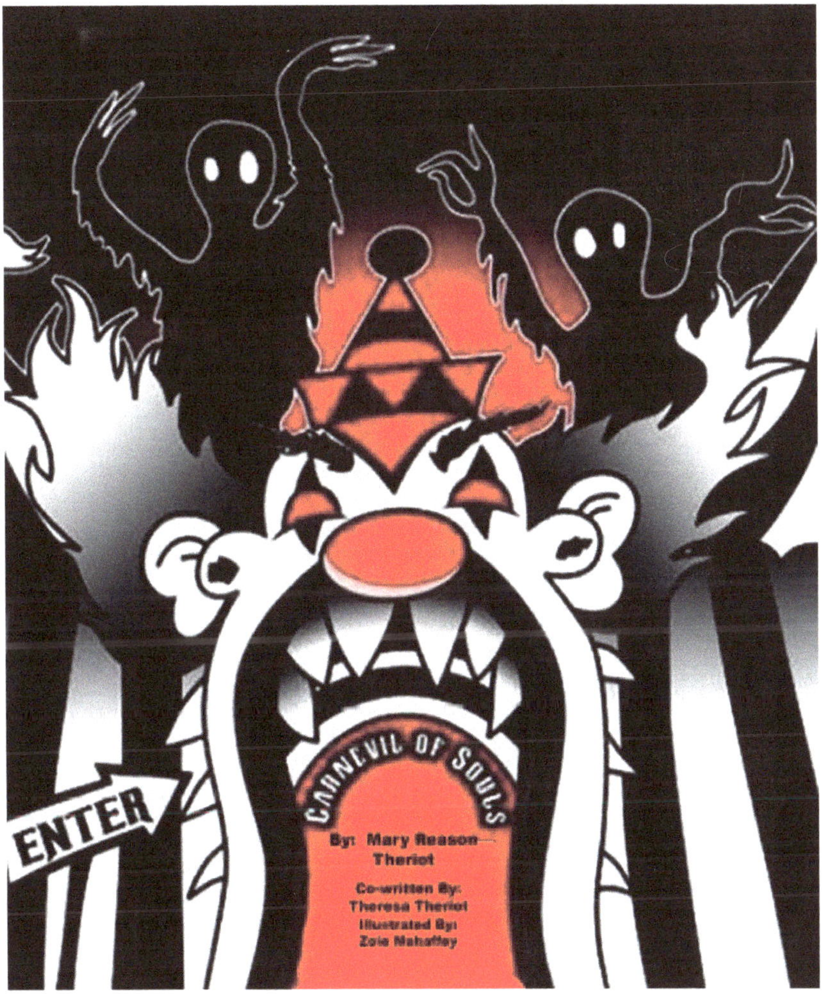

ENTER
CARNEVIL OF SOULS
By: Mary Reason—Theriot
Co-written By: Theresa Theriot
Illustrated By: Zoie Mahaffey

CarnEvil of Souls
Where Darkness Reigns

Book 2

Joshua's Story

By: Mary Reason Theriot

Co-Written By: Theresa Theriot

Dedication

Without the love and support of my family and friends I would not have pursued this new path in life. I would especially like to thank those that have proofread copy after copy, to give me their honest opinion of the books.

To my daughter Theresa, thank you so much for your continued encouragement. I enjoyed every minute we worked together on this book.

To my wonderful husband Malwen, your continued love and support mean the world to me. I don't know what I would do without you in my life. All of my books wouldn't be what they are without you pushing me forward.

To my fans, I would like to offer a special thank you for your continued support.

Acknowledgement

To Adele Hartman for helping to keep the website current with the constant change of information. No one could ask for a better friend and confidant.

To Angel Payne Reason for all the hard work you put in on this book. I thoroughly enjoyed working with you and Theresa. I can't wait to write another book like this one.

Thank you to Zoie Mahaffey, Tracie Landry, Cheryl George and Louie Dupuy for taking the time to let me bounce ideas off of you, no matter how far-fetched they may have seemed at the time. I appreciated each and every one of your suggestions.

A special thank you to Zoie Mahaffey for the wonderful work on all of the illustrations in the book

Dear Reader,

There are some characters that I loved so much that they had to be brought back. *Where Darkness Reigns* contains some of my favorite characters who had to meet and join forces with other characters.

Bianca Honore's story begins in <u>A Deadly Combination</u>, but when she partners with Joshua Savoie in <u>Seduced by Voodoo</u> you learn that her heart and soul are just as black as the voodoo she practices.

Joshua Savoie's story begins in <u>CarnEvil of Souls</u>, but, as in life, true evil never dies but remains hidden until the opportune moment. Joshua comes back in <u>Seduced by Voodoo</u> to see his diabolical plan come to fruition.

Rayne Simoneaud is betrayed by her lover, Dominic St Germaine, in <u>A Deadly Combination</u>, but seeks out her revenge in <u>Seduced by Voodoo</u>.

Josie Bellows is a young vamp from <u>CarnEvil of Souls</u> who searches for the vampire who turned her so that she can find <u>Redemption</u>.

Detective Grace Hutcherson has fought vampires in <u>CarnEvil of Souls</u>, survived the battle of good versus evil in <u>Seduced by Voodoo</u> and now finds herself plagued by <u>Haunted Visions</u>.

***

CarnEvil of Souls – Joshua's Story
A Deadly Combination – Bianca's Story
Seduced by Voodoo – Lovers Unite
Redemption – Josie's Story
Haunted Visions – Detective Grace Hutcherson's Story

Copyright © 2013 by Mary Reason Theriot

ISBN-10: 1-945393-22-X
ISBN-13: 978-1-945393-22-8

Also Available by Mary Reason Theriot:

The Hideaway

The Traveler

Dr. Frankenstein

Above Suspicion

Horror in the Night

Deadly Seduction

Echoes on the Bayou

Seven Deadly Sins

A Kiss So Deadly

A Deadly Combination

www.maryreasontheriot.com

Introduction

Welcome to the CarnEvil of Souls - Where fear never sleeps.

Beware of the trapped souls inside.

Be sure to visit the "DarKastle of Freaks" and the "Maze of the Tortured Fun House."

For a heart pounding thrill ride stop and take a trip:

    Doom Buggy Bumper Cars
    Bone Crusher Roller Ghoster
    The Brain Scrambler

Are you ready for a night of terror under the big top?

CARNEVIL

CarnEvil of Souls' Menu

Come one, come all, and join in the fun. The CarnEvil of Souls is only open at night. Do you dare enter this land of illusion? Be sure to stop and get you something to eat while here. The food is to DIE FOR!

The special of the night is – Gray Matter Platter.

Be sure to check out Billy Bob's BBQ Shack:

> Zombie Barbeque Ribs
> Gravedigger's Roasted Bone Marrow
> Road Kill Pulled Remnant Sandwiches with Zombie Sauce
> Hot 'N Spicy Bat Wings

Don't forget to satisfy that sweet tooth at Hagatha's Sweet Treats:

> Witch's "Poison" Candy Apple
> Deep Fried Lady Fingers
> Corpse Reviver's Lemonade with Eyeball Ice Cubes
> Swamp Juice Snowballs
> Chocolate Covered Rat Brains
> Thorax Cake Pops with Rat's Blood Icing
> Vampire's Kiss Cotton Candy
> Monster Munch Popcorn

There is also the Spare Parts Café that has something for everyone:

> Eye of Newton Kabobs
> Ghostly Good Tongue on a Stick

And for a soul satisfying meal, there is also Carnivore's Meat House:

Gut Filling Sausages
Bloody Good Weenies
Hearty Black and Blue Burgers
Off the Head Club Sandwich

Prologue

Present Day

Everyone loved when the carnival came to town. Parents handed over their happy children to the ride operators without a second thought. They knew nothing about this person; yet they trusted their child's life with them. They had no idea if they were a predator, if that psychotic looking clown handing out balloons was in actuality a serial killer, or something far worse; still they gladly handed over their most prized possession.

Come daylight, a carnival would be revealed to this sleepy town. Rides, booths, and the big top decorated in various shades of blacks, grays, and reds proclaimed their arrival. As with their prior destinations, they arrived unannounced in the middle of the night. Opening night would be filled with the sound of laughter and screams as kids and adults alike enjoyed the rides, games, and entertainment. The carnival would be here for exactly two nights, Friday and Saturday. Come Sunday morning, they'd disappear just as mysteriously as they arrived.

The entryway gates announced what was to come; "Experience the Thrill of the Tortured Souls!" and "Thrills and Terror, The World's Largest Haunted Carnival" depicted what could be found within these confines.

Behind the entrance whipped the canvas flaps of the big top tent where it revealed what would take place; including the freak side show. There was also a fun house with trick mirrors and mazes to get lost in. Be careful not to venture down the wrong corridor or you may find yourself in the "Hall of Tortured Souls" from which you might never return.

The ride operator called out over the noisy crowd, "Who is brave enough to try this ride? Come on folks don't be shy, step right up! This ride is sure to be the talk of the town for years to come." The sales gimmick worked; there was a line a mile long of anxiously awaiting brave souls who wanted to see what the hype was about.

Instead of waiting for the line to die down, the operator repeated his catch phrase, "Come on, young man, I know you are brave enough to ride the Bone Crusher Roller Ghoster. Get in line and be prepared for the thrill of your lifetime."

The young boy looked up at the drop and shook his head, deciding to start off small before moving to something like this. He wondered just how they got the ride so high in the air.

Not deterred by those unwilling to try the ride, the operator continued, "Surely this town has a few brave souls ready to take a seat and try one of the most thrilling rides of their life!"

Chapter 1

Bayou Bend, Louisiana
September 1915

The glowing red handwritten letters across the entrance
way announced the carnival. Up above, the constellations
and bright moon dulled in comparison to the attractions.

The master of the carnival, Joshua, stood in the shadows,
taking in the children's laughter. The tiny town of Bayou
Bend, Louisiana had plenty of people that wanted to leave
behind their worries, even if only for a short time, at his
carnival.

With so much going on in the world, the carnival coming to
town was what they needed. With the war and the struggle
to survive, he couldn't blame them. A smile formed on his
face as he thought about his true intentions. If they knew
what really happened here, they would not be so eager to
spend their money.

He watched as the exhilaration of the carnival transformed
the children's faces. He stepped out of the shadows to
welcome the public to HIS celebration.

Having just feasted on the blood of his latest victim, no one
could see his true self. Instead, they would meet a good
looking man in his late twenties, who was tall and muscular.
He kept his dark hair cut short and the black suit he wore
had been custom made to fit him to perfection. The shirt
was blood red and made from hand spun silk and his boots

were even spit polished to a lustrous shine. His very presence commanded their attention. Soon, one of these unwilling mortals would be his early morning snack. Even after having fed, he still craved the warm, coppery taste of blood.

Almost absent-mindedly, he rubbed the only piece of jewelry he wore. A ring specially created for him years ago. The design resembled a large bat more than a man. He had it designed by one of his family members decades ago. As the soul collector's hunger intensified, Joshua could feel the power of the ring surge through his body, causing the black diamond eyes to glow. His devilish-laugh echoed through the night. After all it was his ingenuity that imprisoned the creature in the ring.

"Hello good townspeople of Bayou Bend, Louisiana. Thank you for allowing me the chance to entertain you and your families. Please enjoy yourselves." His voice practically hypnotized those around him. They stared at him as if in a trance. He could instruct them to surrender their souls to him and they would do so willingly. However, he found no pleasure in that; he preferred the challenge of the hunt.

Stepping back into the shadows, he watched as the crowd rushed off to find games to play and rides to enjoy. He'd recently added a ferris wheel. Its construction took a great deal of time since it was primarily made of human bones. In the center of the large ride was a reflective mirror in which the trapped souls remained to power the massive machine.

He watched as the crowds drank in the attractions. Despite how he felt about these mere mortals, he did feel pride when they looked at his carnival with awe. As tight as their money was, they had no problem spending it here. Even the food vendors were busy. He could smell the money, and of course the fresh blood, in the air. Each of the game operators dressed elaborately to keep the public entertained and entranced.

By the time the locals realized that evil had touched their town, the carnival would be long gone.

Chapter 2

New Orleans, Louisiana
February 1920

Josephine Bellows, Josie for short, had to react solely based on pure instinct. She had a split second to decide. The only thing she could do was run.

The icy cold rain felt like needles piercing into her skin, but she still pushed on. Her bare feet were frozen, and her mind was numb to all but thoughts of surviving.

Darkness ominously descended on the land. What little moonlight was present barely filtered through the trees. The deeper she ran into the woods, the darker it became. She quickly hid in some dense underbrush to stop and listen. Suddenly she realized how eerily dark it was in this area. Looking back in the direction she came from, her heartbeat quickened as sinister shadows moved in closer to where she was hiding. The darkness seemed to devour everything in its path.

Her surroundings became enveloped in a thick, inky blackness. Without regard to her safety, she took off into the unknown; she feared what was chasing her more than what she was running towards. She tripped and stumbled along the way, cutting her leg. Caring not, she pushed on. She refused to give her pursuer the chance to catch her. The ground was slick from the wet leaves that covered the earth. She could hear her pursuer catching up and frantically picked up her pace. How was he onto her movements so quickly?

The cut became painful as the realization of her situation became terrifyingly apparent. The nightmares that had been plaguing her were coming true. She ran to not only save her life, but her very soul.

As she pushed on, her body grew desensitized to the brutal elements and unforgiving terrain. She shivered violently, not from the cold, but from fear. She ignored the bite of the wind that howled through the trees. She refused to think of the immense pain that ravaged her body and threatened to consume her. If she wanted to live, she must run. If she gave him the chance to catch her, she would either die or become one of them. Death would be better than joining the walking dead.

Pure revulsion of what could happen to her pressed her forward. She could hear her pursuer catching up to her. Dread settled deep into her soul as she realized that this was where her nightmares had taken place. She refused to accept that this was her fate and ran faster. She must make it to the river; she would rather catapult herself into the icy water than to die at his hands.

As she neared the river, she swore the tree limbs became outstretched arms with long, boney fingers reaching for her. The gnarled fingers clawed at her and tore away at her already tender flesh and ripped clumps of hair from her scalp. Still, she pressed on.

Her predator was closing in. His breathing echoed throughout the dark forest. His grunts sounded animalistic. They were horrendous and reverberated through her very soul.

With blind determination, she ran faster as she summoned every bit of will she possessed. Her body screamed in protest, but she refused to slow down. With absolute volition, she pushed herself beyond the brink of collapse. Her lungs were on fire, ready to burst at any moment. Hot tears flowed down her face, mixing with her blood. Bile churned in her stomach, moving its way up. She swallowed it back down as she fought the urge to fall to her knees and vomit; yet, she still pushed on, refusing to give up. There was something much worse than death at stake and she refused to give him the chance to make her one of his. The pain that she was suffering right now was nothing compared to the horror that her life could become if he caught her.

What remained of her nightgown was drenched from the rain and sweat; it clung to her body and made it difficult to run. If it weren't for decorum, she would rip it off her body and run nude through the forest. However, she didn't want her body to be found mangled and naked in the river by strangers.

She felt him behind her. The air around her changed as the evil radiated from his very being. The malevolence that lurked inside of him was tangible. Not looking back, she leaped into the air and prayed that she struck the water before he reached her.

She screamed out in desperation as he grabbed her before she could jump. She could not stop the fate that she had dreamed of these last few nights. There was no hope left for her, she was too weak to fight him. No one would come to save her. The life she knew was over. She prayed that he killed her, drained her body of its very life force and did not turn her.

Josie bolted upright and found herself in a strange bed. It must have been a dream, but where was she? She heard footsteps approaching and watched as the door slowly opened. When she saw Joshua, she sighed, "Oh, Joshua how did I get here? I had such a terrible dream."

Joshua came and sat on the bed, "Ah, my sweet, sweet sister. It was no dream."

She looked at him, "Cher, you must be mistaken." Giving him a confused look she asked, "Why do you call me your sister?"

"The master told me he has been intruding on your dreams of late, for that I am sorry. You must know that I did not wish this on you. I will make sure that you are treated well. You can live here with our master or you can come with me."

She gasped, "The dreams, they were real? He truly is a monster?"

Joshua let his hand caress her cheek, "Cher you are to be the same monster as him and I. In time, you will come to embrace your future. There is so much to teach you that Master never taught me."

She shuddered at the thought of living her nightmares, "I cannot live like this Joshua. You are not a monster; I would have seen that in you."

He bent down and kissed her on the forehead, "Cher, you must rest. The transformation is not complete. Soon a ravenous hunger will take over, and then I will find you something to eat. I must teach you to hunt. Our master sees no reason to teach those he has turned how to survive in this world."

This was too much for Josephine to absorb. She let out a groan and threw the covers over her head; she did not want to hear anymore. He leaned over to the lump in the bed and patted her gently. "You must rest now. We will talk more cher."

***

Joshua wished the master had not turned her. But he would ensure that she had everything she could ever wish for. Long ago, he stopped caring for these foolish mortals, but Josephine intrigued him.

He had secretly watched her from the shadows. Had the master turned her so he would have someone on this earth that he could care about? Joshua no longer believed that was possible. His heart had turned to stone long before he had been turned.

Chapter 3

Jackson, Mississippi
November 1926

The Granger sisters gleefully skipped along while they giggled at the various sights. They had never seen anything like this carnival that their parents had brought them to. Who would have thought that something like this would come to this sleepy little town?

Not only were they allowed to stay up past dark, but they could play as many of the games and ride as many of the rides as they liked.

The hum of the Model T engines somehow drowned out the music that played throughout the carnival. Occasionally the honk of a car reverberated through the air.

The sisters stopped to look at the grand carousel. They stared in awe at the reflections in the mirrors and horses that were black as night. The sound of children's laughter filled the night air as the melody entertained everyone. The platform of the carousel went round and round as the horses bobbed up and down to the music. All around, jovial people forgot about their worries.

Fathers hoisted happy children onto their shoulders as they purchased them tufts of pink and red cotton candy. The aromas of roasting hot dogs and popping popcorn filled the air.

***

Elizabeth looked over at her sister, Evelyn, and whispered into her ear, "Randy is meeting me over by the fun house. Can you cover for me if Mom and Dad come looking?"

Evelyn gasped in surprise, "Are you going inside with Randy Evans?"

Giggling Elizabeth exclaimed, "I may even let him hold my hand in the dark."

***

As Elizabeth walked towards the fun house, a repulsive smell overwhelmed her. She didn't know if she wanted to go inside if it smelled this bad on the outside.

Randy came up behind her and whispered in her ear, "Let's go for a walk instead."

Elizabeth smiled up at him, "Okay."

He pulled her towards the dense shrubbery that bordered the moonlit forest. As they walked down the small foot trail, the silvery moonlight barely trickled through the canopy of tree limbs that were devoid of leaves.

***

Curious as to why Elizabeth lied about going to the fun house, Evelyn followed them into the woods. She hoped Elizabeth didn't plan on doing something that got her in trouble with their mom and dad.

The deeper they moved into the forest the less light there was to shine through the heavy branches of the trees overhead. Evelyn was thankful for the heavy blanket of leaves on the ground that kept her footsteps hidden as she moved in closer to where they had stopped. There was no telling what Elizabeth would do to her if she found out that Evelyn was following them.

For a moment, Evelyn thought she heard something behind her and turned around. Not noticing anything, she turned back around when she heard Elizabeth scream. Suddenly, Randy and Elizabeth weren't alone. Randy sneered at Elizabeth while another guy grabbed her from behind. Without thinking, Evelyn hollered out, "Leave her alone!"

Two more boys appeared from the bushes, one grabbed Evelyn as she went to save her sister. "Oh look fellows, we got lucky. There is more than enough to go around."

Evelyn saw the fear in Elizabeth's eyes as the boys forced them onto the ground. Elizabeth kicked and fought in desperation to break free as Randy pulled up her skirt.

Both girls had tears streaming down their faces. Why would Randy do this to her sister? He was handsome and could have any girl he wanted.

As Randy loomed over her, Elizabeth's face became ghostly white. Evelyn's whole body shook in fear and her heart felt as if it would pound out of her chest at any moment.

Evelyn squeezed her eyes shut, attempting to block out the inevitable as her sister screamed in agony, "No, please stop!"

Before any of the boys could make a move, a rumbling bark shook the earth. The frightening sound brought a brief respite of relief. The boys stood up and listened, almost frozen in fear.

As they looked around for the beast that made the noise, it gave Evelyn the opportunity she needed. She kicked herself free and ran to her sister. The girls huddled together as the sound of leaves rustling became more distinct. Evelyn wondered what size dog was headed their way as she could hear the beat of its paws against the damp earth. Attempting to escape the dog's thunderous approach, the boys fled.

Before the boys could escape, a pack of dogs, or wolves to be more exact, broke through the clearing and pounced. Behind the wolves were two men clad in black. Evelyn and Elizabeth watched in horror as the dogs ripped the boys' throats open, spewing blood everywhere.

Evelyn was too afraid to say anything as the men picked the girls up and threw them over their shoulders. The sharp fingers dug into her shoulder as a man hoisted her in the air with unnecessary force. Another man shouted to the wolves, "Heel."

The wolves stopped and watched the man who gave the order, waiting for further instructions. He spoke once more, "Leave no remains."

At once, the dogs devoured what remained of the boys. Evelyn felt darkness come over her.

***

When she woke up, relief washed over her as she heard the music from the carnival in the background. These men must have somehow sensed that something was wrong and came to their rescue. As they neared the carnival, she made out the carousel and the ferris wheel. Where there had once been heavy crowds was now almost devoid of people. The lights and music still filled the night air; yet no one seemed to be nearby.

As they made their way through the mazes of rides and games, Evelyn's heart caught in her throat. These men were bringing them into the fun house. The repulsive smell almost made her gag. She had a feeling they were not bringing them here for a private tour.

Evelyn tried to get Elizabeth's attention, but she was still unconscious. If only she could be as lucky. The men dropped them on the floor, and Evelyn scampered back against the wall as another man emerged from the shadows. All she saw was the glow from the tip of his cigarette.

He walked over and looked at the two girls before informing the men, "Hmmm, this town doesn't have much to offer, does it? You can feed on them."

After witnessing how the dogs devoured the boys, Evelyn's fear escalated. She closed her eyes and waited for death to take over her body as a man picked her up and bent her head back. Fiery pain radiated through her veins when he bit into her neck. As her life ebbed from her body, she felt skeleton hands reach for her soul, drawing it into the depths of the mirror. She stared into its eyes—they were black as coal. It spread its massive wings as its sharp claws dug into her skin. She wondered if the creature in front of her was the Grim Reaper. She felt her very soul being sucked out of her body as its skeleton hands latched onto her. The pain was unending, and she hoped she didn't have to endure this for eternity.

***

Joshua had lured this creature here with the promise of souls. He captured the creature of Satan long ago, along with many others that helped complete his collection. They were bound to this world to do his bidding. They trapped souls for his own desires too. These tortured souls powered the carnival, but he kept some for himself. As the girls' souls, and the creature, were sucked into their prison behind the mirror, it let out a scream straight from the pits of Hades. Once more it tried to break free of its confines, but alas, it could not.

***

Evelyn and Elizabeth's parents panicked. For the last hour, they had desperately searched for the girls, but found no sign of them. Their father, not wanting any more time to pass, told his wife to continue looking as he rushed to find the sheriff.

A search party was formed immediately and the woods and surrounding area were thoroughly searched. No area of the carnival was left uninspected, but no trace of the girls could be found.

Chapter 4

Bloomington, South Carolina
November, 2002

Late November brought two pleasant surprises to the sleepy little town of Bloomington, South Carolina. An unseasonably warm front had settled across the town, and a carnival arrived in the middle of the night.

This was the first time a carnival had come to town, and everyone was talking about it. The children had Thursday and Friday off from school for Thanksgiving, and now they had something to keep them out of trouble.

There was no notice announcing a carnival. It appeared in the middle of the night and set up in record time. It twisted, looped, and spread itself over the land. Banners, lights, balloons, and streamers formed its perimeters. An array of rides and games anxiously waited to be filled with people.

No one questioned why the carnival set up on the outskirts of town instead of in the town center. The morning air was heavy, as though the sun was afraid to show itself. No blue graced the sky; there was only a drab slate-gray slab that looked as if it was ready to go into hiding.

At the dinner tables, kids wondered if there would be clowns, rides, and games for them to play. Come seven o'clock that evening, after dinner had been eaten, cars poured into the makeshift parking lot in search of open spots.

The rides and tents appeared worn and weathered. Could it be by choice or age? No one knew for certain. The antique carousel had black horses with glowing red eyes. In the center of it was a cylinder of mirrors. The awning covering the carousel had a unique look to it, almost resembling aged flesh. A sign at the entrance to the carousel stated, "Beware of the Tortured Souls Inside!" The ferris wheel that overlooked the whole town appeared to be constructed of human bones.

Anxious children pulled their mothers and fathers along, ready to enter. Several children ventured here on foot, not wanting to be seen with their parents.

Ben Davis was one of those children. He called out to his best friend, Frank Myles. "Come on, Frank! Hurry up!"

Frank let out an exasperated sigh, "Ben slow down. It's not like the carnival is going anywhere."

Ben hurried ahead of his friend, money in hand, "Mom and Dad told me I have to be home by ten-thirty. I want to ride as many rides as I can."

Frank groaned, "Why didn't you just tell them you would spend the night over at my house? My parents would have let us stay out longer."

"Mom said that we have to go to my grandparents' house tomorrow to celebrate Thanksgiving there. I don't know why we couldn't do it at our house."

Frank pondered that for a moment, "I don't know dude. Just think, you get to eat two big meals."

"I suppose, but I would rather not have to drive there. It is so boring, and my sister whines the whole time."

After they had purchased their tickets, they walked around the carnival in awe. Everywhere they looked, there were rides and games. In the middle of the carnival was a large tent with a hand painted sign, "DarKastle of Freaks". Ben pulled Frank over to the tent, "Come on, I want to see what this freak show is about."

Frank whined, "But the rides! We don't have all night."

"Aw, come on Frank," Ben exclaimed. "When will we ever get a chance to see a bunch of freaks like this? Aren't you even curious about what could be inside?"

Trailing behind his friend, Frank replied, "Oh, all right, but then we go straight for the rides."

Ben smiled back to his buddy, "Deal. Let's go."

They gave their tickets to the attendant and headed into the dark tent. There was a bearded lady, a rubber man who could contort his body in various positions, but the most intriguing was the wereman. Ben was drawn to it; he wondered how they managed to get him to look so real. He kept asking Frank, "Do you think he's real?"

Frank scoffed at him, "There is no such thing as a werewolf. It's just a prank. Come on, let's go."

Ben looked back at the creature and swore the wereman's eyes just glowed red. He had never seen anything like this. It has a man's body, but the face had been contorted to resemble a dog, and hair covered his entire body. It was not like human hair, but instead, it was like a dog. Ben couldn't explain It, but something about the wereman bothered hIm.

Shaking off the eerie feeling that the wereman was staring at them, he followed Frank out to the rides. The two boys were having so much fun that neither paid attention to the time. When Ben finally noticed it, he told Frank, "Aw man, I am going to be in so much trouble. It's almost midnight."

Frank grabbed Ben's wrist and let out a moan, "Come on, we can cut through the woods and save some time."

Ben looked at the dark woods and shook his head, "I don't know, man. I'm not sure that is such a good idea. We don't even have a flashlight."

Frank let out a laugh, "Don't tell me you are more afraid of the dark than being grounded by your dad?"

Ben admitted that Frank had a point. Not only would his dad ground him for at least a month, but he would probably tan his hide too.

As soon as they stepped into the dark woods, the atmosphere around them changed into something sinister. They were about fifty feet in when Ben started to fear that something was behind them. He called out to Frank, "Did you hear that?"

"It's just the wind, dude. Come on, we don't have that much further to go."

Ben looked around to gather his bearings and followed behind Frank. He hoped Frank was right, and this was the way back home. They had both walked these woods hundreds of times in the daylight, but he had always feared the woods at night.

As they made their way through the dense woods, they both stumbled along the way; falling over a rut or two and overgrown roots. In the distance, the boys could see the lights of the subdivision where they lived and prayed their parents were fast asleep. Suddenly, two dogs jumped and pinned them to the ground. Ben stared at the glowing red eyes of the dog and swallowed down the fear caught in his throat. He knew this was the wereman from the freak show.

Before the boys could react, there were two men laughing down at them. Frank looked at Ben and saw the fear in his eyes. Neither boy had the chance to scream before they were picked up and drained of blood. The vampires threw the remains to the hungry dogs for them to devour. The older of the two instructed the dogs, "Leave no evidence behind, you hear me?"

Instead of answering, they just growled at the vampires as they devoured the fresh meat.

***

Sheriff Darren Murphy swore he was dreaming of a phone ringing. His wife Melissa was shaking him, trying to wake him. "Darren, the phone is for you."

He took the phone from her, "Murphy."

"Sheriff, I hate to wake you in the middle of the night, but I have some extremely worried parents here. Their children went to the carnival last night, but they were supposed to be home by ten-thirty."

Sheriff Murphy looked over at his clock and saw that it was two o'clock in the morning, "Maybe the boys weren't paying attention to the time and stayed longer than they were supposed to."

"Yes, sir. That was what I said. The boys' fathers thought the same thing and went to the carnival to look for them. They didn't see them there."

Sheriff Murphy pulled himself out of bed, "Get a search party together. I am on my way."

***

By the time Sheriff Murphy arrived at the Police Station, the search party had been organized. Ben's parents, Hank and Marion Davis, along with Frank's parents, Greg and Jenny Myles, were pacing back and forth in the front office.

As soon as Greg saw Sheriff Murphy open the door, he rushed towards him, "This isn't like the boys. I figured they would stay a little past their curfew, but it is two in the morning. They should have been home by now."

Sheriff Murphy placed a hand on the man's shoulder, "We will search the woods to see if maybe they took a shortcut home. They may be lost and can't find their way out. Don't worry, we will find them."

Mrs. Myles stood frozen by the window, silently crying as she stared out into the darkness. Sheriff Murphy's heart went out to both sets of parents, but he had a feeling the boys were goofing off and not paying any attention to the time. The carnival had everything the kids were excited about. He suspected that quite a few would miss curfew tonight and stay until the doors closed at three o'clock in the morning.

***

Out in the woods, the search party looked for the boys. Sheriff Murphy divided the volunteers into groups, and they branched out, calling out their names as they went. They walked slowly through the dense undergrowth as they made their way to the clearing that led to the carnival. The woods were full of creatures moving tonight. Up above, birds circled as their rest was disturbed by the noises. Rabbits and deer scampered out of their hiding spots, bolting before they could be seen. The search party continued to comb the woods as the Sheriff, and several officers made their way to the carnival.

Sheriff Murphy walked over to the ticket booth operator. "We have a report of two missing boys from the area. They were supposed to be here and haven't returned home."

The ticket master looked at the photos before handing them back to the sheriff, "They could have been here. We have had more than our fair share of kids tonight. Go on in and look around."

"Thanks so much."

***

Joshua watched as the police officers moved about. He stepped out from the shadows, "Hello officers. Is there something I can help you with?"

Sheriff Murphy looked at the imposing man, "We have a report of some missing children and wondered if they were here."

He smiled at the officers and waved an extended arm over the area, "As you can see, there are children everywhere. Please feel free to search the grounds. I can have some of my men help if you like."

Sheriff Murphy shook his head, "That won't be necessary." He handed the man pictures of the young boys, "These are the two we are looking for. If you see them, please tell them that their parents are worried, and it is time to go home."

"Of course Sheriff. I will have one of my men personally escort them home if we find them."

The police officers and Sheriff Murphy searched every square inch of the carnival grounds, finding neither hide nor hair of either young boy. As Joshua watched the cops leave, the smile disappeared from his face. He quickly walked into his trailer as his alpha dog followed close on his heels. Once inside, the shape shifter took human form and awaited further instructions. "I am glad to see that you are on time tonight. We have performed our last show in this town. I don't like that a disappearance was discovered so soon after our arrival."

***

Morning came quickly. When the sun was fully risen the last of the rides had been broken down, and the caravan was ready to leave.

As the search for the boys continued, Sheriff Murphy found it strange that the carnival left in the early morning hours and had not stayed their allotted time. He made a few calls to find out more about this mysterious carnival.

Chapter 5

Grand Junction, New Mexico
December, 2002

It was the beginning of December when the caravan of trucks and trailers turned on Highway 25 and headed into New Mexico. Sunset fell on the state as the sun glared off the top of the buildings. Most of the crew were still sound asleep, but they would soon be awake and ravenous.

Tyler noticed that Josie was waking up. He had always had a soft spot for her and had often wondered how she became involved with this bunch, but he must guard those thoughts carefully. The repercussions would be life ending if he did not. He watched in awe as she stretched her long, lean legs, making her way out of her hiding spot.

He had lost count of the years he had been her protector. He often wondered if she sensed his crush on her. After all, their senses were keen, and they usually could read minds. If she knew, she had never once acknowledged it.

One of these days, maybe he would find the courage to approach her; like that would do any good. Vampires didn't fall for shape shifters. In all the years he had known her, he had yet to see her fall for anyone. For a while, he suspected that she had a crush on the master, but lately he noticed the way she glared at the master when he wasn't looking. No, he doubted she had a crush on him. Perhaps she didn't have the courage to leave him and this group. Truth be told, none of those following him were brave enough to leave him. Leaving was a death sentence. Once you were in this family, you were there permanently. There were too many secrets that he didn't want to be revealed. Although the shifters weren't privy to everything since he treated them like they were dogs, he had heard whispers and had seen things while the master slept. There was much more to this place than a traveling carnival. It was the true epitome of evil.

As Josie kept to the shadows, she asked, "How much longer before sunset?"

He replied, "The sun is going down as we speak."

She smiled, "I couldn't sleep any longer. I am so tired of traveling. I am ready to get out and smell the fresh air."

"This had been a longer haul than normal. It was imperative that we put some extra distance between us and the last place."

The Sheriff in the last town they had stopped in was quicker than most. He had come right up to the grounds and started looking just a few hours after the young boys went missing. Generally, when someone went missing, the local law enforcement agency made those filing the report wait forty-eight hours. The master had been wise to leave; no one wanted to be discovered. This has been their way of life for too long. They had lived for decades hiding undercover in the carnival. They didn't want to be forced to change their lifestyle.

***

Josie drowsily looked out the heavily tinted rear window at the all too similar terrain. It seemed as if they had been traveling this area for the last several months even though they hadn't. She had grown tired of the wanderlust. She wondered what it would be like to settle down in one place and not see the carnival day in and day out.

The only problem would be telling Joshua. Something told her he wouldn't take kindly to her wanting to leave this life. She looked over at Tyler and knew she couldn't leave him. She had never once told him that she had feelings for him for years. That was if a vampire could have feelings for someone.

At that moment, Tyler looked back in the rearview mirror and caught her looking at him. Her breath caught for a moment; could he be thinking of her too? She smiled at him and dismissed the idea. He probably considered her as one of the charges that he must protect. Certain vampires in the family had a personal guardian and private trailer. The others shared trailers and a guardian. Joshua, and only Joshua, chose your standing in this family. He made sure that they all knew the pecking order.

Tyler asked, "Did you sleep well?"

She nodded her head, "Mmm hmm. I'm just restless."

He knew the feeling. At least they would be in New Orleans in a few months and once there, they would stay longer than just a few days. There they could take a moment to roam and cut loose.

***

Josie stepped out into the night air and took a deep breath. The sun had finally set, and the stars were coming out.

For decades now, she had followed Joshua; followed his every command without question. She had been loyal, completely devoted to him. Only, lately, her feelings had changed. She could no longer follow his evil tasks and sadistic whims. She felt guilty taking the lives of the innocent.

The hunger took over her body, making her skin crawl and her fangs twitch. The need for blood always remained present and always strong. She had come to loathe it.

She watched as the others came out of their trailers. They would all feed tonight; some would take lives instead of merely feeding. She wished for a life where she didn't need blood to survive. She would feed, but she would hate every minute of it.

She despised what her life had become. It was such a perverted, dark existence that she now lived.

Chapter 6

The carnival always arrived without warning. Announcements never preceded its arrival; no flyers, no advertisements in the newspapers, no billboards - nothing. It simply was not there when the town went to bed and when they woke, there it was.

The towering rides, the big top tent, and the games were almost devoid of any color. That did not concern the citizens of this small town. They couldn't wait for the carnival to open. By the afternoon, everyone would learn of its arrival. And by nightfall, word would spread to the neighboring towns. Word of mouth was always a more efficient method of advertisement. People couldn't stop talking about the mysterious carnival that appeared out of nowhere.

Once the gates opened, people would pile in and marvel at the rides, games, and food. There was still an hour before opening, but crowds were already forming outside the gates.

No one questioned why the carnival only opened from nightfall to dawn. They naturally assumed it added to the carnival's intrigue. The only movement inside was a slight rustle when the wind blew through a tent. While it looked abandoned, if you smelled the air, you could catch a whiff of the hot dogs and popcorn.

The crowd became restless from waiting. As the sun dipped below the horizon, movement started from the back of the carnival. The night sky came alive with lights from the rides and music filled the air as the carnival came to life.

Children's laughter could be heard as the gates and ticket booth windows magically opened. The carnival was officially open for business.

***

A group of teenage boys stood on the hill that overlooked the valley below. Sean, the oldest and, therefore, the leader, asked Jared and Max, "What do you guys think?"

Jared kicked at a stone on the ground, not wanting to sound like a wimp, but he did not want to go on the rides, "It looks lame to me."

Max scoffed at him, "Dude, you need glasses. That place looks totally rad."

Sean shook his head, "I agree with Max. That place looks totally rad. Instead of cheery colors, it is decked out in black and red. That is cool and so goth."

Jared just looked at his friend. Sean had recently become infatuated with the color black and all things goth. He'd even tried to talk them into filing their incisors to resemble fangs. "Oh, all right, if y'all want to go I guess I will too. If this turns out to be lame, I am outta here." As he made the statement, he was already heading down the hill to the valley. The other two followed close behind him.

Jared was the newest to the group. His family moved to the little town of Netherland, New Mexico only a year ago. He still missed the big city, but he was finding that living here had its perks. Now that he had found some friends to hang out with, he didn't miss his other friends as much; besides, he and his old friends still talked on the computer at least every other night.

He had been to other carnivals in the past, and he wasn't impressed. He despised the rides and kiddie games. They were lame, but if he wanted to stay with this group of friends, he would ride the rides and hope they found the games as boring as he did.

As they neared the carnival, he noticed how this one differed from the others he had been to. It didn't have any of the bright colors, and it was also the biggest he had ever seen. There were a lot of trucks and caravans parked around the perimeter and more rides than you could count on your hands. He noticed a ferris wheel, a carousel, a roller coaster, and a fun house. There was also an enormous tent set up in the middle of the property. He wondered what was in there.

As they walked around, deciding which ride they wanted to hit first, Jared took a glimpse at the games, half expecting them to be childish. He was proved wrong. He wondered how much money this place brought in nightly. He imagined what the life of a carnie must be like. It must be nice never having to stay in one place and not worrying about your future. You traveled the country with the caravan and saw all the sites. This could be the perfect life for him. Who was he kidding? The carnies probably wouldn't welcome him either.

Jared heard Sean let out a whistle, "Man, this place must rake in some serious dough."

As soon as Max caught a glimpse of the fun house, he yelled, "Dudes let's go in there first."

Jared would rather not do any of this, but he figured the fun house was better than the rides, "At least, the line seems to be moving fast."

As they stepped in line to wait their turn, Sean muttered, "The rides will be better than this. It's probably lame. I mean you don't even hear any screaming coming out of this place. It's probably nothing but a maze of mirrors and plastic skulls."

Jared was glad to know that he wasn't the only one who would rather not go through the fun house, but he kept his mouth shut. A carnie worker dressed in black with the most fantastic pair of fangs took their tickets. Jared wanted to ask him where he could find a pair like that, but before he could speak, his friends shoved him inside.

Sean let out a laugh, "Did you check out the worker? He is so not doing the goth thing right." Jared looked over at Sean. Sean was just jealous that the worker had goth down better than him. Once the door shut behind them, they were enveloped in darkness. Jared couldn't put his finger on the smell, but it was atrocious, almost as if something was decaying.

Max noticed the same thing, "Dude, they really need to clean this place. It reeks."

The black lights helped to illuminate their way. Jared felt something cool on his legs and saw a heavy mist covering the floor. They must be using dry ice to give it a creepy effect. He had to admit, it worked. Skulls and crossbones adorned the walls. Jared thought that Sean was wrong about the bones looking plastic—they seemed real to him.

***

Joshua lurked in the shadows, watching Jared. He might be the perfect addition to the family. His level of self-importance was extremely low. It would be easy to mold into something he could control. The friends with him he had no desire for, except for food.   He was careful not to bring in someone too strong willed to control, but he didn't foresee that being a problem with this boy. Besides, with the carnival growing, they needed more strong workers.

The master instructed one of his girls, "You see that young man moping about?"

"Yes, sir."

He told her, "I want you to turn him. He is perfect for the family. The other two you can dispose of as you wish."

She bowed to her master, "As you wish sir. I will get right on it."

Chapter 7

Harrington, South Carolina
May 2003

Joshua woke with an unquenchable hunger for that sensual blood. There was such an intimacy in drinking and killing as if it were a heart to heart dance. As a victim weakened, he felt himself strengthening as he consumed their very soul. He became infinitely more powerful than any other vampire who ever walked this earth with each soul he took.

Lately, the taste of mortal recognition had become too seductive. He wanted to be the symbol of evil in this world and beyond. Even with his increasing powers, some days he swore an impending doom was following them - which was ridiculous. No one even knew they existed.

Vampires looked like humans, even the old ones. With the flip of a collar and dark shades, most humans wouldn't even give them a second glance. If they did, all they needed to do was send them a little telepathic razzle dazzle, and they forgot their existence. Maybe, this was fate telling him that it was time to proceed with the next phase of his plan. That may end this edgy feeling that he couldn't shake.

Perhaps a walk would calm this restlessness; besides, he needed sustenance. Tonight, he wasn't in the mood to feed with his children. He needed time alone. He dressed in his favorite disguise: A form fitting black leather jacket, tight black jeans, and a pair of black boots that were good for walking on uneven terrain.

When he looked at his watch, he noticed the time. He'd slept later than normal. With a sinister smirk, he realized it would mainly be drug dealers and criminals out roaming the streets. When they turned up dead with no known cause, the police would blame their lifestyle and dismiss the deaths without a second glance. He could simply feed off of them, but there was no fun in that. Besides, he would be doing the world a justice by removing them from the streets. Their souls would be his to consume, and not to power the carnival.

Lately, he had felt a sudden increase in his powers. His speed was faster, and if he didn't control his psychic ability, he could read the thoughts of people within a ten mile radius. He had also noticed his improved night vision. He wondered if his own children's powers had strengthened. He would have his guardians pay special attention to them and inform him at once if they felt he should be concerned about a particular child. They were supposed to use the souls they collected strictly for powering the carnival, but it only took breathing in one soul to find out what it could do for you.

The carnie life was perfect for him. He preferred the life of a wanderer. He despised staying in one place for any length of time, and that was how he ran his carnival. They left town long before anyone ever realized that someone was missing. They had traveled to various cities and towns in the United States, but in Canada and Mexico too.

Yes, he liked being the master of this carnival. He could do whatever he liked, whenever he liked and answered to no one. He had more money than any one person could ever spend in a lifetime and created the perfect hunting ground for his fellow immortals. He liked having his family with him. It was crucial that he keep his grand coven close; that way he ensured they did not get careless.

He never made excuses for what he was or why he did what he did. He was a creature of the night, but was also more. Others like him did not realize just how special their powers were and everything they could actually do. He, however, refused to let those powers go to waste.

Some felt remorse for killing, but he did not. Did humans feel remorse for killing cattle, pigs, chicken or other meats for their supper? No, they had to eat the same as vampires. It was pure and simple logic.

Over the years, or rather decades, Joshua had looked pure evil directly in the eye. While he may be perceived as evil, he was nowhere near as evil as some of those he had met.

He had accepted the fact that he was a vampire and had no desire to be mortal again. He left that life behind a century ago.

He had no plans to find an alternative to human blood and had no wish to seek out a blood bank. His long life had taught him not to be ignorant of what went on around him. Over the years, he had honed in on his incredible skills, and they had served him well.

He was currently learning how to use his powers to control the human mind and not just read it. After consuming a few more souls, he should be able to commandeer that power.

Vampires were predators. When the carnival came to town, he and his children hunted. While some of his children only sought out those they believed deserved to die; he did not.

Even after a century, he remembered the day he had been turned as if it was yesterday. He had been out hunting, foraging for something to eat when he had heard a rustling in the woods. The sight he stumbled upon did not scare him as it should have. Instead, it intrigued him.

When the creature stopped feeding it turned to Joshua, "You do not run in fear?"

"Mais non, sir."

"You are from New Orleans, oui?"

"Oui, my family is from here. We live along the bayou."

The creature wiped his mouth, "And why, pray tell, are you out tonight?"

He looked at the creature, still intrigued by what he witnessed, "I was hunting for fresh meat for tomorrow's meal."

"Well, mon ami, I am sorry that you happen to be out on a night such as this. For you see I cannot allow you to live and tell others about me."

Joshua, not being scared of what the creature was saying, replied, "And exactly what are you? I see that you have feasted on this harlot who worked in the Quarter."

The creature moved closer to him and smiled, making sure that he revealed his fangs, "And you still aren't afraid?"

"Why should I be?"

The creature replied, "I am a creature of the night, a vampire."

"So, you are the walking dead?"

The creature gave a wicked grin to Joshua, "Ah, so you have heard of my kind?"

"Only in fairy tales are the likes of you mentioned. Mon ami, this is New Orleans, and I have learned that much can happen here. My mere constantly worries the slaves are practicing voodoo; yet, she still refuses to free them."

"Your mere may be right. She would be wise not to turn a blind eye on them. I find you intriguing, young man. Perhaps I should turn you into a creature of the night. Would that be of interest to you?"

Joshua pondered what he was asking. The thought did not repel him, "Yes, I would like that very much. For you see, I believe that there is more to this world than what we see."

The creature exclaimed, "Ah, my son, there is so much more to this world than what you have experienced. What you are to become has its limitations. You will be a creature of the night. There will be no more sunrises for you, no more walks along the river to soak in the sun, and you will be limited to walking in the night air."

He let out a laugh, "I am already a night owl. My pere always fussed at me for sleeping all day and playing all night."

"And your pere, will he come looking for you?"

"Mais non, my pere died unexpectedly. My mere believes the cook poisoned him. He was a mean man, very cruel to the slaves."

"And your mere? Will she miss you?"

Joshua let out a cruel laugh, "Mais non. She is too worried about her own neck to be worried about the likes of me. That is why I am out here hunting. She refuses to eat anything the cook prepares for us. She swears that the cook poisons it."

 "I take it you live on a plantation, then?"

"Mais oui. It is one of the smaller plantations. It only consists of two thousand acres."

"And if I turn you, we can stay at the plantation? No one will bother us?"

Joshua shrugged his shoulders, "Just my mere lives in the house with me. The cook refuses to live in our quarters. She would rather sleep on the floor in the kitchen."

"Take me to your plantation. Once I see it for myself, I shall decide if I will kill you or make you a child of the night."

"It's not too far from here." Joshua led the way; he was amazed that the man following him hadn't once asked him to slow down. He could obviously see better in the night than Joshua, who had walked these grounds countless times.

The man observed the plantation from a distance and saw no other properties were nearby. "Yes, this will do nicely." Before heading closer to the house, he bent Joshua's neck back and sank his fangs into the tender flesh.

***

Joshua awoke the next day to find himself in his bed with the heavy curtains drawn. It took him a moment to realize what was waking him; his mother's pounding on the bedroom door.

"Joshua Savoie, you better have killed us something to eat. I am in no mood for your shenanigans today, cher. I just know the cook has poisoned our breakfast, and it is going on lunch time. I must eat, I tell you."

He assumed last night must have been a dream, but when he went to get out of bed, he felt too weak to move. He threw the covers over his head and fell back into a deep slumber ignoring his mere's pounding on the door.

***

His new master, though, could no longer take the incessant pounding and made his way from his hiding spot under the bed. He opened the bedroom door and looked at the dreaded woman who his new child called mere, "Woman, you are insufferable." Before she could respond or even scream, he pulled her into the room and made a snack of her. Once he had drained her of her blood, he licked the puncture wounds clean and watched as they disappeared. With a flick of the wrist, he threw her clear over the railing of the stairs. When her body was found, they would think she either jumped or that the cook finally killed her. Either way, it made him no mind. He was happy to be rid of her. She would have made his life miserable.

***

Joshua awakened several hours later to one of the slaves screaming. He managed to leave the room without the light hurting his eyes too bad, but he still felt weak. Leaning on the banister, he asked, "What is the problem?"

The housekeeper cried out, "Your mere, she is dead."

He saw his mother's body, but he could not bring himself to feel any emotion from her death. He instructed the housekeeper, "Have someone bury her next to Pere and leave me be. I feel horrid."

***

Joshua stayed in his room for several days. He felt his body changing, morphing into something different. He found that as long as he left the heavy curtains drawn and his door remained locked, he didn't feel as weak. When the sunlight hit him, he would rather die than suffer through more. He could tell when dusk was near; he felt stronger, more powerful. He also felt his features changing; his fangs were growing.

The cook left him food at his door, but it didn't satisfy his hunger. No matter how much he drank, he couldn't quench his thirst. For a moment, he thought he was going insane; he heard voices, but he soon realized he was hearing everything the slaves were thinking.

The seventh night brought an unending hunger. He heard footsteps coming near his bedroom door and his senses were immediately assaulted with the smell of heavy perfume and something else; it was something he'd never smelled before. It had a coppery scent that caused his fangs to throb.

The door creaked open, and the man from the woods walked in. He had with him a harlot from the Quarter. His master looked at him and said, "It is time to eat."

Before the girl could let out a scream, he was ripping at her throat. His fangs sank into her artery and he drank, as if by instinct. He tore off her dress in record speed, exposing her milky white skin. He ripped open her body with his hands and found her internal organs. He devoured them whole without even thinking of what he was doing. An ecstasy came over his body like nothing he had ever experienced before. Finally, his hunger was sated.

Joshua and his master lived at the plantation feeding and enjoying their life for over a decade. It was easy to dispose of the bodies on the plantation, but Joshua wanted more from life. He bid his master farewell and began to wander. The only problem with wandering was disposing of the bodies. That was how the carnival came about. He was able to grow a true family and dispose of the bodies easier. They hid under the cover of the carnival, and their food came to them. A butcher that he had turned suggested using the bodies as food for the mortals. He had some old family recipes and from there they started making sausages and hamburgers.

The only time Joshua saw his master was when he returned to New Orleans. Sometimes he came to visit Joshua, but those times were getting few and far in between. That was fine with him; he didn't want his master to witness what he had become. He would be disappointed to discover that his child had turned so evil, so diabolical. However, he had no wish to return to his former self.

Chapter 8

Augusta, Washington
December, 2004

They moved under the cover of the darkness of night. Only a pale sliver of a moon was out. Even the stars in the sky remained hidden. It mattered not; they didn't need light to help them see. Lurking about at night kept the attraction off of them, but the truth was that not one of them could go out in the daylight even though they desired it more than anything else. A few have tried to cover their skin with sunscreen protection, but even with the highest SPF, the sun blistered their skin. He loved the night; it fit him. Here, he was the master of his domain.

The convoy formed a complete circle around an abandoned construction site. Joshua looked around, pleased with the space. He knew this was the perfect place to set up when he saw the holes dug out for massive pilings. They easily disposed of the bodies that belonged to the souls of those they had taken.

In one corner of the property sat several abandoned pieces of construction equipment, several bags of cement, and other expensive supplies left behind in haste. Joshua smiled wickedly at this find. *Yes, this would be an excellent place to set up.* They didn't even have to work hard at hiding the bodies. They could dig a hole and before leaving, fill it with the cement. Since the freezers were full, meat was not in great demand. They still had to be careful how many souls they took over these next couple of days. He did not want their presence to be known.

As he gave the signal, the trucks stopped in formation. Workers flowed out of the vehicles and quickly went to work putting the carnival together. The Big Top went up first, the rides and game booths soon followed suit, and the food vendor booths were last. They hung the banner announcing the opening on Friday night at eight o'clock sharp.

By daybreak, everything would be set up and ready for their grand opening. The tent was fully equipped with everything needed to amaze and amuse the crowds, all the while they could find their supper. They required a few fresh souls to regenerate the power that ran the carnival. With this being the last week of December and school still out, the children should flock to the carnival.

He woke the shape shifters. While the carnival traveled across the country to their next destination, they slept throughout the journey. The pack was small, but as master of the carnival he had had them under his charge for decades now. They finished cleaning while the carnival workers slept. During daylight, the shape shifters ensured that they were safe and kept out any curious onlookers. At night, a few preferred to roam the grounds in their true form. They were the most spectacular wolves he had ever seen. The alpha male was raven black with gold eyes that glowed red when he was angry.

***

Nearby, Sally Graham and Blake Crowley were in a field when they heard the commotion. They stopped their current activities to see what was going. Both were surprised to see the rides go up. Nothing had been mentioned around town about an upcoming carnival. She wondered why he had not informed her. A carnival in this small town was huge.

Wanting a closer look, she pushed him off of her. He let out a moan, "Come on Sally, surely you don't want to see a dumb old carnival more than me."

"Hush up Blake. This is huge. Dad didn't say anything about a carnival coming to town."

"You are killing me Sally. You can't just bail on me."

She gave him a smile, "Let me see what is going on and then we can get back to what we were doing. Besides, if there are carnies around here, I do not want them to see us."

Sally watched Blake sulk on the way. She only dated him to get back at her parents. She despised her parents sometimes. They may be rich, but they were weak. Her father was the president of the largest bank here in town and her mother was nothing more than a social butterfly who headed various committees. The only time they seemed to notice her was when she went out with Blake. She knew that she was a disappointment to them; she was not the beautiful and graceful daughter they desired. Her mother wanted someone who she could dress up and show off to her friends at her social gatherings. Instead, Sally was tall, skinny, and very awkward.

One day, she overheard her mom blaming her dad for the way she'd turned out; she informed him that Sally resembled his side of the family. That was the day she stopped loving her parents and started to make their lives a nightmare instead. She had made them pay not only in monetary items, but with mental anguish too.

***

They moved quietly to the back of the tent, listened for any noises, and watched for any sudden movements. As soon as they found a good hiding spot, they saw a tall, dark man dressed in black walking towards them. Blake watched with curiosity as the man appeared to smell the air. He wondered what that was about.

The next thing he knew the man moved quickly to where they were hiding. He had no idea how the man moved so fast, but he put a death grip on both of them. He held them up off the ground and peered right into their very souls. He heard Sally whimper, but there was nothing he could do. The more he struggled, the tighter the man grasped his neck.

A sinister smile appeared on the man's face, "Welcome to my carnival; unfortunately, we are not open for business, but if you would like, I can show you around."

Sally nodded in agreement, and the man dropped them both to the ground where they landed with a thud. Blake was glad that for once Sally was keeping her mouth shut about who she was and how she shouldn't be treated this way. He had a feeling this man wouldn't care. Before leading them inside the tent, the mysterious man peered into the darkness to see if anyone else was watching and ushered them in.

Chapter 9

Joshua looked at his supper and watched as the man pulled hard at the restraints. He noticed the man walking around the carnival tonight looking at the young children. As soon as he entered the man's mind, he saw what the man planned on doing this evening. This man made the perfect supper.

He called for his alpha dog and gave instructions to lure the man to his trailer and keep him there until he could feed.

Throughout the night, he felt the man's fear building and sensed his strong will to survive. *"Yes,"* he thought to himself, *"This man's soul would be perfect to strengthen my powers."* He learned a long time ago that souls as black as his gave him the most power.

He'd lost count of how many souls now inhabited his shell of a body. When he took a person's soul, their memories and knowledge also became a part of him. Those souls gave him his power, his life force. A few believed that they were stronger than him and attempted to overtake his mortal mind. He merely laughed at their futile attempts. No matter how many souls he possessed, his soul remained the strongest since it was the blackest.

As with all vampires, Joshua needed blood to satisfy his bodily cravings, but he also needed so much more than that now. He found himself craving more dark souls. His hunger was not sated until he consumed the blood, the spirit and soul from the victim's body.

He watched as his charges feasted on the warm blood of a corpse. When they finished feeding, he moved in before his soul catchers claimed the soul. He stared deep into the blank, frozen eyes of the dead as he breathed in their soul.

The soul, or aura, was the true life in the mortals, not the blood. The body was just a shell for that life force and energy. As death set in, the life force detached from the body. He had watched death enough times to see the moment that life left the body. As the shell took one final breath and a last heartbeat, the soul departed the body. That was when Joshua claimed the aura.

***

Before Josephine went to bed, she must talk to Joshua. Maybe if she spoke to him and explained how she was ready to settle down, he would understand and give her permission to leave. She subconsciously rubbed the mark on her wrist. Joshua branded his children so that they remained connected to him. It reminded them that they were bound to him forever.

As she entered his trailer, she found him in the middle of the floor kneeling over a body feeding. The sight would be permanently imprinted in her mind. As the apparition left the body, Joshua inhaled it. From the aura surrounding it, this soul must have been black-hearted. It had a black shadow in the center of its being. She often wondered how he captured the souls, and now she'd witnessed it first-hand.

As she looked at Joshua, shirtless and covered in blood, she noticed a flicker of evil in his eyes before it disappeared. What caught her attention was the transformation in his face. It was as if his physical appearance changed as his body absorbed the gangrenous soul that it just collected. Could this be the cause of Joshua's demeanor? Did the evil he fed off of change him? Would this happen to her if she continued to feed on the dredges of society? She shook her head in disbelief; no, she didn't collect their souls for herself; she took the blood and left the souls for the soul collectors. Let them be consumed by the evil that lived in their black hearts.

Josie had known Joshua for so long, and it disturbed her to witness what he had become. He'd taught her so much; showed her a world that she never knew existed. Without him, she could not have survived her transformation. He was the one who taught her how to stand on her own two feet and when to lean on friends. He taught her how to read people and how to have self-confidence in everything she did. Since being turned, she had learned that life was short and way too precious to take for granted. She had also discovered the true beauty of death. While she had once feared death, now death would be such a sweet release from this life.

She saw the anger in Joshua's eyes as soon as she walked in the room. "Why didn't you knock?"

She stammered, "I came to talk to you for a moment. I didn't mean to interrupt you. I am sorry."

He stood up and walked towards her, "Let me clean up and then we can talk."

Unable to see anymore, she shook her head, "That's okay. I can talk to you later."

"Are you sure? It won't take me long to clean up and have the Rougarou come get the body."

"No, really, it's okay. I just wanted to talk. It's been a while since we just sat and talked."

He looked at her suspiciously, "Are you feeling okay?"

She felt him dig deeper into the recesses of her mind, so she let her mind go blank as if she was just relaxing and wanting to talk. "I am fine, really. I am homesick for Louisiana."

He took her hand in his, "We will be back in Louisiana soon. If you are that homesick, you can always stay with our master. I am sure that he would love to see you."

She just shook her head. Once she was turned, he'd left her with Joshua. She had no desire to see the man who cursed her very existence.

Chapter 10

Greensborough, Texas
January 2007

As he walked the streets, he reveled in the scent of the soft, fragrant humans walking by. He loved the fact that the living didn't notice him in the slightest. The air was humid tonight; rain hung heavy in the air. The sky had a dark, polished look to it as the silver moon sat high in its place.

Men and women rushed about him as they attempted to beat the impending rain. The hiss of the wheels of a passing bus drowned out the noises of the city. The large streetlights winked in the darkness of the night.

He continued to wander down the street as a breeze picked up debris and blew it carelessly around. There was a flower vendor still working, arranging flowers for tomorrow. A butcher was closing his shop after a busy day. Newspaper vendors hurried to fill their machines. Several bars were packed with mortals seeking alcohol to forget their troubles.

Joshua entered the all night diner in search of a midnight snack. He sat down at the bar and looked around at the various patrons. He had hoped to find a few strung out teenagers for a midnight snack, but the place was almost empty.

He assumed the old man sitting at the back table was homeless. From the way he nursed his cup of coffee, he must be looking for someplace to sit for a while. He looked as if a gust of wind could pick him up and carry him off and Joshua wondered when the old timer ate last.

Taking out his wallet, he pulled out a twenty and called the waitress over, "Have that gentleman over there order something to eat and pay for it with this. You can keep the change. Let me know if you need more."

The waitress looked surprised, but responded, "That is very kind of you. I didn't have the heart to kick him out. The poor man looks as if he has been down on his luck for a while."

He nodded his head in confirmation. If he had given the old man the money outright, he might have pocketed it for booze. This way he knew he would get something to eat, which was more than he could say for himself at this moment. The old man wouldn't provide him with any sustenance. There was no telling what impurities were in his blood. He could smell the decay in the surrounding air and doubted the old man had too many more days on this earth as it was.

As he continued to look around the diner, he did a double take. He didn't know how he'd missed her the first time, but there in the back corner sat a young girl picking at a very rare steak. He sniffed the air and could tell that she was the same as him. He decided to walk over and see what her story was. She must be newly turned if she was trying to eat a rare steak or perhaps she had something against the real thing.

As he walked over to her table, a bunch of rowdy teenagers walked in and sat at one of the front tables. This group would make the perfect snack. Instinct had told him this place would be a good source for food, and this group of boys was just what he had a taste for. They were full of life, hopes, and dreams. The air was charged with the energy emitting from their bodies. When he looked at them, he wondered what their dreams were. Did they think of their future or did they just think about getting stoned and laid?

***

She watched as the hunk of a man moved towards her. He stopped and looked at the rowdy bunch that just walked in. Their obnoxious laughter grated on her nerves tonight. She looked down at the plate in front of her with longing. She wished she could just pick up the plate and lick every last drop of blood on it. She suffered from a hunger that never seemed to be fulfilled.

She hated the poison that ran through her veins. As much as she despised the need to feed off of humans, the guilt that washed over her afterwards was far worse. She tried to avoid the human world as much as possible, but tonight the hunger had become too strong. She had walked into this diner, hoping that the rare steak would help curb her appetite.

Now, a man who was total eye candy was heading her way. This was not what she wanted and she groaned inwardly when he arrived at her table. No matter how good looking he may be, she had no desire to listen to the ramblings from anyone right then.

He looked down at her and asked, "Do you mind if I sit here?"

She responded, "I am really not in the mood for company tonight." As she was telling him to buzz off as nice as she could, the obnoxious group of boys let out a loud chortle of laughter. The sound reminded her of fingernails being raked down a chalkboard. She rolled her eyes at the noise.

He pulled up the chair across from her and sat down. As he kicked his feet up on the table, he lit a cigarette. She stared in awe at the smoke from his long cigarette. It was black as his hooded eyes and the clothes he wore. As he lifted his cigarette to his mouth, she noticed the neatly trimmed and pale nails. Once more he pulled on the cigarette and blew black smoke. He told her, "I think you will want to talk to me. Don't worry; I won't keep you long. If you don't like what I have to say, you can send me away."

She looked at him with weary eyes and shrugged, "Something tells me you won't take no for an answer."

He let out a deep laugh, "I knew the minute I saw you that you were a smart girl." He held out his hand and introduced himself, "My name is Joshua."

"Ashley." When she caught a whiff of him, her instincts went into overdrive. Could this man be one of them? She learned that there was an odor to them. It wasn't overwhelming, but a hint of a scent there.

He asked her, "What are you doing out in this area so late at night?"

She just sat there and stared at him with a forlorn look. She couldn't explain it, but he made her feel comfortable. It had been a long time since she felt at ease with anyone.

"I could ask you the same thing."

He gave her a wicked smile, "You can say that I am a night person."

She narrowed her eyes and continued to look at him. He smiled at her as if there was no double meaning to what he said. Could she be mistaken?

She let out a soft laugh before responding to him, "You can say that I am a night person too." She waited to see if he caught the double meaning of what she had said. This was the one thing that she never joked about. She had not adjusted to the change in her lifestyle. She attempted to befriend others like herself only to be shunned.

She waited for him to make a snide comment, but instead, he just glanced at the steak in front of her. When he looked back up at her, it shook her to the very core. He was looking at her with sympathy in his eyes. He knew her secret.

He told her, "I can help you with the transition if you want." She looked up at him with complete surprise in her eyes. He went on, "There is so much that I can teach you. You need to hone in on your abilities; for instance, you can read minds if you are taught correctly. I can also teach you how to eat. Eating like you are right now will not satisfy you. Am I right?"

She slowly nodded her head in agreement, afraid to speak. When she finally found her voice, it sounded shaky, "Who are you?"

"I am like you Ashley. I am a vampire, a very old vampire. I can help if you let me."

She nodded in acceptance, and he replied, "Well, why don't I help you get a real meal tonight?"

Unsure if her voice would betray her, she nodded once again. He told her, "That rowdy group is getting ready to leave. Why don't we go and get us a bite to eat?"

She replied with regret clear in her voice, "I am not good at feeding."

He chuckled softly, "Well, this will be your first lesson then."

When they stepped into the night air to follow the boys, the damp humidity clung to them. Up above, the moon hung low with only a few of the brightest stars penetrating the inky black sky.

As they continued on their way, he went on, "First off, I need to tell you about some of the old wives tales that have been passed down to keep us protected during vampire hunts. Holy water has little to no effect on us, also we will not burst into ashes from the touch of a crucifix, but it will sting. You see, years ago, vampires relished hunting humans more for sport than food. Packs of vampires raided villages and slaughtered everyone who lived there. A group of vampires united and labeled themselves the High Council. This particular group of vampires feared that our existence would be found out and unanimously ruled that the butchering of humans must come to an immediate end. There were those of us who did not like that this particular group had been formed and continued killing for sport. This upset the High Council and they subsequently formed their own special law enforcement group to deal with those who refused to obey their rules. This elite force of vampire hunters leaked out rumors to the public on how to ward off vampires so that they could hunt them in private."

"Do these vampire hunters still exist?"

He nodded his head, "Yes, this elite group still exists, but if you hunt properly, you will never bring your existence to their attention. This is what I will teach you. Now, if you prefer not to feast off of fresh blood, I can show you which blood banks to visit. However, I do not find the blood nearly as satisfying."

***

As they headed back to his place after eating, she asked, "How did you know about me?"

"As I told you earlier, we have the capability to read minds, among other things. If you stay with me, I promise to teach you everything you need to know about your new life. I can show you that there is more to being a vampire than you realize."

She looked at him warily as he continued, "You do not have anything to fear. You will be safe."

Instead of responding, she continued walking with him, contemplating what he had said. All she had planned to do tonight was sit in the diner and attempt to curb her hunger while wallowing in self-pity. Now, here she was with someone stating he could help her after all this time.

When they passed a small café on the corner, she caught a whiff of the coffee and beignets that still lingered in the air. She longed for the days when she could taste the hot beignets and café au lait. There was something about the messiness of the beignets and the powdered sugar that got everywhere that she craved. Not long ago, she'd walked into a diner that served beignets and ordered a plate full hoping it would satisfy her hunger. As soon as she bit into the crisp doughnut, she felt disappointment swell up inside of her. The taste had repulsed her instead of it hitting the spot.

Waiting for her answer, he informed her, "You must learn to trust your feelings and go with your instincts. If your gut is telling you to listen to me and join my group of vampires, then you should. If it tells you that you shouldn't go anywhere with me, then that is what you should do."

His offer was tempting. It was what she had longed for, to be welcomed by others like her instead of hiding among the living. With them, she would not have to fear if they touched her. They wouldn't question why she was so cold to touch, as if she wanted to be reminded that she was a walking corpse.

As they neared the carnival grounds, the scent of fear and fresh blood mixed heavily in the air. Her fangs slid out instinctively as she smelled the air one more time. Even though they had just fed on the rowdy bunch of teenagers, hunger built inside of her once again. Someone had recently fed here; she looked at her new friend to see if he mentioned anything, but instead, he kept walking, passing through the gates of the carnival.

She closed her eyes and tried to listen to her senses as he had instructed. She could not hone in on anything that might have taken place here. As she peered into the night, all she saw was darkness. She closed her eyes tightly to see if she could fine tune her hidden senses. When she opened them once more, she still saw nothing but the inky blackness of the night. All she heard was a throbbing noise that seemed to resonate throughout the grounds. The air was charged with an energy that she suddenly noticed. Someone alive was here and felt genuine fear. This was a carnival, and understandably some feared the rides.

Joshua whispered in her ear, "Try one more time to sense what happened here."

She closed her eyes once more and really concentrated on the area. She sensed the fear all around her now. People called out for help, but the voices seemed to surround her. An image appeared before her; it was a scared young teenage girl backed into a corner. A figure appeared before her and instinctively she knew it was not human. She watched as he stalked his prey and prepared to feast on her. She felt his delight as he took the girl's life from her. She shuddered in repulsion.

***

Josephine watched from her trailer as the master brought in the new charge and wondered who she was. She had known Joshua for a very long time, and he tended to have a kind heart when it came to those abandoned by their makers

It had been almost a century since her maker turned her. She had been restless one night after having had the same nightmare once again. For a week every time she closed her eyes, she dreamed of her true love coming to her. But he came to her as a horrible creature and not as she knew him. She had tried to shake the dreams off by blaming the rumors that had been circulating around town. People were disappearing and parents had warned children not to venture out at night.

She had not taken heed to their warnings and believed there was nothing to worry about. She didn't think there was anything to the recent disappearances. Two had disappeared on the same night; she believed they ran away together, and the others probably left on their own free will to find a better life than what was here. What had sparked fear in the townsfolk was when Old Man Singleton's cows began to die off from a mysterious disease. He went out to the field and discovered one or two every other night, completely drained of blood. No one believed him until he brought a cow into the center of town to show everyone. That was when the frenzy started.

If only she had heeded those warnings; she shouldn't have gone outside that night to clear her mind. She had loved Joshua ever since she saw him walking about town one night. No matter how hard she tried to throw herself at his feet, he never noticed her. And when he did speak to her, he treated her as a sister.

The dreams had become more vivid and that night she had again dreamt of her own demise. She had hoped the fresh air would calm her soul, but unfortunately, that fateful night was the very night she lost it.

She had prayed he would kill her, but instead, he had cursed her. That was when she learned of Joshua's secret. No matter how hard she tried to eat as Joshua had instructed, the process repulsed her. Late one night, she ventured out of the house to find something to help ease her ravishing hunger. That was when she found the others. They were on the outskirts of town one night feasting on the cows, unsure how to quench their hunger and too afraid to go into town to find food. She went to Joshua and shared with him what she had found. They had wandered the countryside aimlessly until Joshua took them under his wing. That was when he decided to start the traveling carnival.

At that time, she had been enamored by Joshua. She would have followed him to the end of the world and back;

ironically, that was exactly what she had done. Now the guilt tore at her. She was no longer certain about this life. What remained of her human side moved closer to the surface. She was merely an anguished shell of an immortal. She detested what she had become. She had lost count of all the souls they had trapped here in this blasted inferno. And she now knew that Joshua was keeping souls for himself. She suspected that he used them to become more powerful.

She learned how to keep him from invading her mind and finding out what she was thinking. She had to allow him access to some of her thoughts or he would become suspicious.

She walked into the trailer well before dawn, unable to take any more of the night. Only a small amount of the light from the carnival made its way into the dark trailer. As soon as she walked in, she could sense Tyler in the dark.

Josie took in her guardian's hulking figure, the short hair and bulging muscles. Even in the dark room, she could make out the small scar on his jaw and the gold flecks in his eyes.

Tonight the draw to him was too much to deny. For once, she wanted a pair of arms wrapped around her that made her feel safe and secure. She often wondered what it would be like to come home to his open arms.

When Josie ran into his arms, it made him shiver with desire. Heat rose up inside his body.

Josie felt his gaze burning into her body. Did he feel the same way for her?

Without thinking, they both tumbled onto his bed, neither able to keep their hands to themselves. As soon as his mouth took hers, she knew she was his. His very touch took her breath away. His lips claimed hers and consumed her. He nipped her lips ever so gently before parting them with his tongue. She gave herself to him; she was more than willing, ready and able.

She hadn't known a simple kiss could ignite such a fire inside her body. She molded her body closer to him, wanting to be one with him. She couldn't get close enough to him. Neither worried about the consequences, nor cared about social conventions or what others believed. Her vampire heart wanted this shape shifter and nothing else mattered.

Love must reside somewhere in the body other than the human heart as she no longer had one, or a soul for that matter. She was the undead; lately, that mere fact weighed heavily on her mind along with the guilt of what her life had become. She was now feeling a fierce, deep love. She had longed for this kind of passion her whole life.

Yes, love must come from some place other than the heart. No one here could ever learn what went on behind closed doors. She would relish every private moment they had together.

She assumed when she had been turned that her heart had turned to stone too. She accepted the fact that she would never know a lover's touch, but when Tyler kissed her, she felt herself wanting so much more out of her life.

Could she convince him into running away with her? There had to be a place they could find sanctuary. She worried what Joshua would do to them if he ever found out.

Tyler sensed that Josie was miles away in her mind, "Are you having regrets?"

She shook her head, "No, absolutely not. I wanted to be in your arms. I have wanted this for so long my love. It's just that I hate having to keep this a secret from everyone."

He kissed her one more time before looking her in the eyes, "I know. Don't worry, we will figure something out."

She cuddled into his embrace, "I have grown tired of this carnival life. It's just that I can never let Joshua know."

Tyler agreed, "We have to be careful. You must keep your thoughts guarded."

He took her lips in his once more and she lost herself in his sweet embrace.

Chapter 11

Jessup, Texas
February 2007

Amber Williams was ready for this school year to be over. However, it was only February and she still had a few more months to go. As she walked to school, she heard someone yelling, "Hey Amber, wait up!" She groaned when she saw Chris Haskins walking her way. He had pestered her for over a month to go out with him. She was done with boys. She was almost seventeen and ready for a real man to show her a good time. She wanted someone who talked to her and listened to her dreams. She was tired of these boys who talked about nothing but themselves and football. As soon as she graduated, she intended to move far away from here.

Chris started jogging to catch up with Amber; his lean, athletic body was evident under the tight t-shirt and jeans that molded his body. "Hey Amber. I was wondering if you heard that there was a carnival in town."

This caught Amber's attention. She hadn't heard about a carnival coming to town, "A carnival is here in THIS town? For real?"

"Yep. It is set up right on the outskirts of town, near the old Hanson place."

She couldn't contain her excitement, "That is so cool. I've never been to a carnival before."

"A bunch of us are going tonight after school. Do you want to go with us? It's always more fun to go to these things in a group; that way, we can share the same ride, you know?

There will be lots of food and some games to play. I bet they will have a show in the big top.”

“That will be totally awesome. What time did y’all want to meet there?”

“We are meeting at the town square at six. It doesn’t open until nightfall so it will give us plenty of time to get in line.”

“Cool. I will see you at six.”

***

By the time they arrived at the carnival grounds, it was almost six thirty. In about thirty minutes, the carnival would open. Amber had expected to see chaos here tonight as they hustled to get everything ready.

As soon as seven o’clock hit, pandemonium broke out. The ticket booth opened and before she knew it, heavily tattooed men and women walked around shouting. Booth operators tested the rides and games as the crowds poured in. When she entered the grounds, the smell of buttered popcorn wafted through the air.

As they walked to the rides, Amber smiled to herself. She was actually having a great time with Chris and the others. At first, she had been unsure of how tonight would go, but now, she was glad she didn’t cancel at the last minute. All of her senses came alive as a gentle breeze blew through the area and caressed her face as it moved past her. She looked up at the multi-colored lights that danced around them. They reminded her of a kaleidoscope that she’d had as a child.

All around them, she heard ringing bells from the rides and games. Several game booth operators were calling out,

"Win the lady a prize!" While the ride operators tried to draw the crowds in their way by hollering, "Ride the Brain Scrambler."

She had never seen so many different food booths. She couldn't wait to delve into the tempting treats that had been teasing her senses with their tantalizing smells. There were corn dogs, cotton candy, funnel cakes, cheesy bacon French fries, onion blossoms, and just about anything you could think of deep fried.

Her sensory level was going into overload, but she loved this carnival. For the first time, she felt comfortable letting her hair down and slipping over to the wild side. She felt completely uninhibited here.

Before riding any more rides, they decided to grab a bite to eat. As soon as they walked up to the booth, Amber felt her heart skip a beat. The man in it was well over six feet tall and reminded her of the clowns crammed into the tiny cars at the circus. There was no way he could stand up straight in the booth. Not only was he extremely tall, but he had muscles on top of his muscles. She bet there were even muscles on the man's ear lobes. She could make out tattoos of a snake, dragons, and some demonic symbols. She knew that you shouldn't judge people by their appearance, but it was difficult not to judge someone who looked like he did. It wasn't the tattoos that bothered her, but the choice of his tattoos. His appearance was made worse by the fact that he had on a "wife beater undershirt" that had seen better days. It was stained yellow from the grease splatters from the food he cooked. It amazed her that he wasn't covered in sweat from the heat of the food booth.

He looked down at them from his perch, "What do ya want?"

As soon as he spoke, Amber wrinkled her nose at the odor that emitted from his mouth. It smelled as if something died inside of him. Barely able to talk, Amber stuttered out, "Bacon cheese fries and a hamburger, please."

"Anything to drink?"

"Um, oh yeah, a soda, please."

He turned away and quickly filled her order. She was surprised that as big as he was, he moved around the small food booth with complete ease. As he handed her the food, he gave her a sinister smile that gave him a wicked look. She didn't want to run into him in a dark alley. She paid the man for her food and hurried away.

She waited over by the end of the line for the others to order their food. Once Chris purchased his food, he remained with her as the others placed their orders. He said to her, "I don't know about you, but that guy gives me the creeps."

She nodded in agreement, "He wouldn't be my first choice to serve food that's for sure."

"I swear when you look into his eyes you can feel the coldness in him."

She shrugged her shoulders as she bit into her hamburger. This had to be one of the best burgers she had ever eaten. The meat almost melted in your mouth. "I don't know what is up with all the tattoos, but he sure can cook a mean hamburger."

As he bit into his greasy burger, he nodded in agreement, "They could put the diner out of business." They had their food almost entirely devoured by the time the others met up with them.

After they had finished eating, they brought their trash to the dumpster before heading back to the rides. As Amber lagged behind her friends, she looked over at the food booth one more time, and a shudder went through her. She swore the man looked right at her with a hunger in his eyes.

He caught her looking at him and gave her a quick wave and a smirk. She panicked for a moment; when he smiled his tongue licked his lips. She swore that his eyes briefly turned red. She grabbed Chris, "I swear there is something wrong with that food man. He is staring at me, and I think his eyes turned red."

He laughed at her, "Don't be ridiculous. You are letting your imagination run wild." Grabbing her hand, he pulled her along, "Let's go see what rides we can find."

As they made their way to the rides, the music from the games caught his attention. He pulled her towards them, "Hold on Amber, I want to give this a try. I have to see if my dad is right about the games being rigged."

She rolled her eyes, but she agreed to watch him play the stupid little game. "Oh, all right, if you have to, but hurry up. I have to be home by midnight, and we still have a lot more rides to try."

Chris gave her a goofy grin and took the sledgehammer from the operator. He stared up at the pole before raising the sledgehammer and swinging down as hard as he could.

The little metal ball skyrocketed to the top of the pole. His smirk turned into a smug grin as he handed Amber a prize.

***

Amber was having fun, but she needed to find a bathroom before going on another ride. She told the rest of the gang that she would catch up with them. She stepped into the big circus tent figuring there had to at least be a port a potty somewhere in here. As she made her way to the back, a dark figure appeared before her. Before she could scream, hands grabbed at her and covered her face. Sharp teeth sank into her neck as her captor inhaled her soul as it left her dying body. He dropped her lifeless body to the ground as his tongue circled his mouth capturing every drop of her blood.

He instructed one of the workers, "Remove her before someone sees it."

"Yes, sir," he replied and carried her body off to one of the back rooms of the circus tent. They would hide it for now and devour it later, when they could enjoy the succulent meat.

The leader of the group reminded the others, "It is almost time to start the show. Remember to be careful in choosing your food; we don't want anyone to get too curious."

***

Grant Harrison watched as the ever growing crowd made its way through the carnival. From every direction, elbows and bodies jostled him as he made his way through the multitude of people.

He noticed Chris standing still, looking around. Grant asked him, "Dude, isn't this place great?"

Ignoring his friend's comment, Chris asked, "Have you seen Amber anywhere?"

Grant shook his head, "No, dude, I haven't seen her."

As they made their way through the crowd looking for Amber, they saw Frank and Sarah up ahead. Both were sharing an overly large tub of popcorn. Even from here, you could see the yellow grease drip from the popcorn carton. Grant could almost taste the popcorn as he watched them greedily eat the tempting snack. His stomach let out a loud growl reminding him that he hadn't had much to eat today.

Grant told Chris, "Let's go find something to eat. Maybe, Amber is over by the food."

Chris shook his head, "You go ahead and call me if you see her. I am going to go check over by the restrooms and see if she is there."

Grant shrugged his shoulders and headed over to the food booths, unsure of what morsel he wanted to try first. The enticing smells were far too tempting to ignore. He planned to disobey his mom's strict diet for the family. He wanted to gorge on junk food.

Besides, he may as well get something to eat since the place was crawling with little kids and their parents. It wouldn't be long before the kiddos were ready to go home and be put to bed. Then the lines would be shorter, and they could ride as much as they wanted.

***

Josie watched as the boys rode the various rides. They reminded her of the youth she missed out on. If only she could warn them to leave this place, never look back, go home, and lock their doors tight and do not to let anyone in.

She could smell the hunger in the air tonight; there would be many souls enslaved. Her other brothers and sisters wouldn't take their fill and simply erase the victim's memory. No, they would drain their body of blood and either throw the bodies to the pack or prepare the meat for sale as food for the mortals.

She had grown tired of this life. It was time for her to move on. She could no longer take the guilt of ending these young ones' lives anymore.

Chapter 12

Chariton, West Virginia
July 2009

The excitement he had been enveloped in all night was quickly replaced with an overwhelming rush of terror. The young boy ran as fast as he could, breathing heavy with every other step. He occasionally glanced back to make sure he wasn't being followed as he hurried through the heavy underbrush. Dense woods surrounded the carnival, but on the other side was the town. If he made it there, someone would be able to help him. He had to tell someone what he saw. They had to be warned.

The woods opened up to a clearing that led right into town. All he had to do was make his way down the small hill. Unexpectedly, he felt a push from behind. As he fell, he searched for something to grab onto as panic set in. By the time he made it to the bottom of the hill, he was covered in dirt and leaves. Not bothering to brush himself off, he scrambled up and took off in a frantic run. He must find help. He must warn the town of what lurked at the carnival. For a moment, he felt dizzy and disoriented, but he shook it off.

He was so close to town. Once there, he would be safe. He would be able to get help. Tears rolled down his cheeks as he thought of what just happened to his friend.

He heard a rustling in the trees, but was too afraid to look back. He kept telling himself it was just a rabbit or deer moving and not someone or something from the carnival chasing him.

Twigs snapped behind him, but still he refused to turn around. He picked up momentum and ran even faster into town. His heart was pounding; his mouth was dry. He could see the street lights from here; safety was not too far away. It would lead him to a small subdivision where he could finally find someone to help him.

As he rounded the bend of the road, he could see the first house. He'd made it. Suddenly, arms reached out from the darkness and grabbed his shoulders. He tried to yell, kick and scream, but he was instantly silenced.

***

Adam Hill never had a chance to warn anyone in town of what he'd witnessed that night; that he had seen his best friend Chad Hale become a vampire's supper. He instead met the same fate. Their souls would be trapped in that carnival forever.

Neither of their parents would know that they had snuck out in the middle of the night to go see the attractions that had come to town. They would wake up in the morning wondering where the boys were, unaware that they would never be seen or heard from ever again.

Chapter 13

Becky Hopkins loved Halloween. She found this time of the year magical. She wasn't sure if it was the spooky decorations or that you could dress up and be anyone you wanted. But each year, she couldn't wait for the Halloween parties and carnivals.

When she was a little girl, she couldn't wait to dress up and go trick or treating. She planned out her costume a whole month in advance and always wanted something original. Her mom allowed her to take old clothes and transform them into her costume. Sometimes she went to the local thrift store and found something cheap to turn into a perfect costume.

This year she and her friends planned on going to the carnival that set up magically in the middle of the night. It just proved her point that Halloween was indeed supernatural. They agreed to dress like vampires. It may be cliché, but she was already making plans on how her costume would stand out from the others. From what she had seen of the carnival from the road, even the workers seemed to be in the festive Halloween mood. Everything was draped in blacks and grays with a splash of red here and there for color. It had a haunted look about it that was perfect.

On her way into town, she contemplated her costume. It, of course, must be dazzling, and it HAD to grab the attention of the guys. Her vampire outfit would be seductive, hypnotic, and very dangerous. A shiver of anticipation rushed through her body as she pictured herself walking through the carnival decked out for the festivities.

As the day went on, more people commented on the carnival. Other carnivals had come to town, but none like this. The secrecy that surrounded it made it even more exciting, and people were eager to go.

No one in the Town Hall seemed to be worried about its arrival, so that helped put people at ease with the mystery that surrounded it. A few concerned citizens had inquired with the city officials and learned that the carnival had requested to set up in town. They asked that it be kept a secret until opening day. It was part of their intrigue and helped draw people in.

***

Yes, this carnival had done its job well, just as it had done over the past century. It never visited the same city twice, that was except for New Orleans. New Orleans was the only city that they seemed to blend in with those who dwelled there; however, even going there had to be once a year as to not draw too much attention to themselves. It was also home for Joshua. Most citizens there couldn't remember anything about what happened during Mardi Gras, which was why they selected that time to visit. Most of the town was inebriated, and those who weren't minded their own business and let those who wanted to party have their fun.

As he stood in the shadows watching the crowd of people forming lines in front of the ticket booth, he chuckled softly. Tonight would be incredible, he thought to himself. It would soon be time for the carnival to open. Once the sun set, they could move about. For now, they kept to the shadows of their tents. He watched as his children prepared for the busy night. Some preferred the brightly colored costumes over the black clothes that he liked. It didn't matter to him. The bright colors helped to distract the general public from their coal black eyes that were devoid of any life.

As the crowd continued to grow, his mouth watered. So many eager people had come to have fun tonight. He smelled the air and could taste their blood on his tongue. No one would go hungry tonight.

***

After slipping into her red stiletto heels, Becky checked herself in the mirror before heading out to meet her friends at the carnival. The heels were the perfect touch for the outfit; they accentuated her long legs and drew attention to her calves. She took a moment to fix her "fangs" that she'd purchased at the Halloween store the other day. These "fangs" felt like teeth and slipped right onto her incisors. The salesman gave her special glue that kept them in place, and when she wanted to remove them, she had a special mouthwash that dissolved the glue. She smiled at herself in the mirror and marveled at how the "fangs" look on her. Doing a quick twirl in front of the mirror, she had to admit that she looked fabulous. The makeup she bought gave her the illusion of a very pale face and her lips were perfectly plumped and red from the special lipstick. She blew herself a kiss as she headed out into the night.

By the time she arrived at the carnival, it was jam packed with people waiting to get in. As she made her way to the ticket entrance, she saw her friends in the middle of the line. Thankfully, someone managed to arrive early to get them a good spot. She only wished it would move faster so they could purchase their tickets and enter.

***

The line moved faster than she had anticipated, and it didn't take long for them to get their tickets and enter. As she looked around, Becky still couldn't believe they'd gotten this place looking this great overnight. They must have worked around the clock preparing for their grand opening. After looking around, she saw why they opened only at night; it helped create the perfect atmosphere. It looked positively evil. Spooky music played in the background, and spider webs hung everywhere. They even had bats flying overhead. Tonight was sure to be a massive hit.

***

He watched with satisfaction as the crowd poured into the carnival grounds. Children ran around screaming and laughing, trying to free themselves from their parents' grasp. Teenagers walked around in search of rides, funnel cakes, and possibly a place to sneak off to for a quick make out session. Those were the ones to watch. They could sample the food before deciding which ones to feed on. Their victims would have no conscious memory of ever having been bitten. It had taken years of practice to develop this trick, but it came in very handy. It also kept the High Council and the public from ever suspecting what was going on at the carnival.

He breathed in the night air. The smell of young blood caused his fangs to come out. He was anxious to sample the lives that were here. As more people entered, the lines grew longer. No one would go hungry tonight. If they did, then it was their own fault. There was a good selection to choose from.

***

It was a beautiful fall night; the air was crisp but not yet cool. Stars twinkled above, and the scent of popcorn filled the air. They passed a vendor cart selling candy apples, and saw the hard red candy glitter like rubies against the flashing lights of the rides. Music played all around her, and carnies yelled out to those passing by in an attempt to get them to play.

One of the booths caught Becky's attention, and she stopped to look at it. There were rows and rows of plastic black cats with glassy eyes and mocking looks that stared back at the players. This game drew people in, all wanting to knock these cats down to wipe the smug look off of their faces. She must admit that they had really kept with the Halloween theme.

Stepping from the shadows, the game operator snarled at her, "You gonna play or just take up space?"

The man was tall and thin. Even though there was a slight chill in the air, he had on a black ribbed tank top that showed off his biceps and heavily tattooed arms. The guy gave her the creeps; the way he leered at her was unsettling. In a huff, she turned to walk away, but one of her friends, Dave, decided he wanted to play. She wondered how this place made any money if the other workers were as rude as this one.

Dave barked out to the worker, "I wanna give it a try."

The rude worker handed him a baseball of sorts as Dave perused the targets. Giving the man a buck he took his stance to throw the ball.

Becky stared at the rows of cats once more, wondering if they knew what was about to happen. She swore they were looking at them calmly, almost taunting Dave that he had no chance of winning. She suspected that the game was rigged. Dave would have to hit them dead center if he had any hopes of knocking any down.

She watched in awe as Dave sent one cat at a time crashing down to the ground. Even the carnie worker seemed to be a little surprised. His grim face barely cracked a smile as he tried to hide his astonishment.

To help draw more players, the worker shouted, "See folks everyone is a winner. Step right up and have your turn."

While talking, the worker swung his arms towards the prizes. It didn't take long for a line to form.

The group took off once again, wandering through the crowd and checking out the sights. There was a merry go round that, instead of brightly decorated white horses, was adorned with sleek black horses with glowing red eyes. Becky took notice of the dark, ominous theme that enveloped this particular carnival. Instead of brightly covered tents, the theme was various shades of black and gray, which made one think they were ancient and had been around for decades. However, none of this bothered the other carnival goers. They were laughing and enjoying themselves immensely.

A ride caught their attention; even from here, they could hear the screams of the current riders. There was something about being scared to death on a ride that thrilled Becky. The ride reminded her of an old tinker toy. The large contraption rose high in the sky. There was a long metal pole in the middle and at the base were eight separate seats that went all the way around. Your feet were made to hang from the bottom. As the base turned, you were brought to the top in slow motion and then plummeted to the earth. After the initial plummet back to the earth, you slingshot high in the air before once more returning. She had never seen a ride like this before and couldn't wait to take her turn.

She noticed how mesmerizing the ride operator's eyes were. They were black as coal and paid no mind to Becky and her friends as they waited for their turn. The ride operator stared out into the crowd, possibly dreaming of being someplace, anywhere else other than here. But, then again, if they knew what was on her mind, they would cringe in fear.

The ride operator finally got up and moved towards the machine to let the riders exit. As they gave their tickets, Becky caught a glimpse of the riders as they climbed out. They appeared a bit pale and wobbled pass them.

As they found themselves a seat, Becky started to doubt its safety. None of the chairs felt as if they would hold their weight. She feared they would fall right through the seat that looked like it was made out of human bone held together with bits of wire. The safety bar felt cold and stiff across her lap. No, she didn't feel safe at all.

As the operator came by to check the bars, Becky swore that she sneered at them. With the flip of a switch, it began to turn. As they made their way to the top, it spun faster.

She held on tight to the lap bar, afraid that she would fly out of her chair. As soon as they reached the top of the ride, it came to a sudden halt and from here they could see the whole carnival. The lights from the other rides flickered below them and from this distance everyone looked like ants. A light breeze blew through and shook her seat as they waited for the next part to start. It seemed like minutes ticked by before the ride moved. When they finally made it back to the ground, all they could talk about was how fast and intense the ride was. So far, it was the most thrilling thing here.

***

As he was about to move to the big top, a tempting morsel caught his eye. He couldn't wait to sink his fangs into her tender flesh. He wondered how many here would join the number of those "missing". He'd given strict instructions to his family not to take in any more new family members. Only he could make that decision.

They were not a "truc" family by blood, but by creation. He chose only those that he wanted to be around. He had a blood family at one time, and he learned that bloodlines did not make the heart stronger. His father was a vile man, and his mother only had concerns for herself. No, sometimes it was better for you to choose your family.

***

As Becky and her friends headed to the other rides, she noticed everyone in town must be here tonight. It seemed everyone had the same idea to dress up in costumes. She doubted anyone was trick or treating tonight.

She was so busy looking around that she didn't realize she had lost sight of her friends and collided right into someone. If he hadn't grabbed her shoulders, she would have fallen flat on her bottom. When she looked up to see who she ran into, she gasped in delight. This was the man of her dreams. He was tall, handsome, and well built. He must love Halloween as much as she did because his costume was the best vampire one she had ever seen. As he held her shoulders to steady her, he captivated her with his eyes. They drew her in. She imagined herself pulling his face down to hers and kissing him. Before she knew it, he walked away and vanished into thin air. She shook her head to clear her mind. Could it be that she'd just imagined the whole thing? No, she knew she bumped into him. She must find him again and introduce herself.

As she made her way through the crowd, she spotted him walking into the big top tent. Suddenly, he turned around and stared at her, long and hard. Her heart caught in her throat as every sensation in her body came alive.

She followed him and pushed her way through the crowd. She was desperate to meet up with him before he vanished into thin air once again.

From a distance, she heard someone call her name, "Becky…. Becky." Instead of answering her friends and heading towards them, she chased after him. She knew in her heart it wasn't the safest thing to do, but she just couldn't let this man slip through her fingers.

Unable to draw her gaze away from him, she continued to ignore her friends calling out for her; instead, she pushed on through the crowd. She must meet him face to face and find out his name.

As she followed, he never looked back to see if she was still there. What was wrong with her? She had never stalked a man before, but she was doing just that. However, she had never seen such a fine specimen as this one.

As she closed the distance between them, she never once stopped to question her reasoning. He could be luring her to her very unfortunate death. She could be following a serial killer.

When she made her way closer to him, he turned around and stared directly at her. She saw the primal interest in his eyes. Even if she wanted to turn and walk away from him, she couldn't do so. A seductive grin curled his lips, and she could see his fangs peek through. She thought how much better his fangs looked than hers.

This man was the first person that had ever had such a profound effect on her libido. She suddenly found herself standing right in front of him. The seductive smile was still on his handsome face as he looked down at her. As she stared at him, she sucked in a deep breath. This man was so tempting.

Her mind was full of arousing thoughts. She couldn't believe he was wrapping those well-defined arms around her body. As he pulled her closer to him, she completely surrendered to his seductively erotic kiss.

When his head bent down to hers, her heart raced in anticipation of what was to come. Her palms became clammy as her mouth went dry.

As soon as he touched her, goosebumps rose all over her body. She gasped in delight as the deep and pleasurable sensation took over her body. His touch was intoxicating.

She was in such a state of bliss that she forgot about the world around her.

The intensity of his kiss heated her blood. Passionately, he claimed her mouth. This was by far the best kiss she had ever had. With just a kiss, she ached for him instantly. He pulled her closer to him as she entangled her fingers in his thick, glorious hair. The desire he felt for her was evident in his kiss.

As his tongue probed deep inside her mouth, his strong hands caressed her back. His touch was exhilarating. He was wickedly sinful. She let out a soft groan as his lips left hers and moved down to her neck. Her last conscious thought was of the prickling sensation against her neck.

Chapter 14

Naples, Arizona
May 2011

As Royce Wells walked up the stairs, he balanced his books
in one arm and dug in his pocket to find his dorm room key
with the other. He let out a disgusted sigh when he got to
the room and found that his roommate had left the door
wide open once again. He wished his parents would let him
spring for an apartment instead of this stupid dorm room.
At least with an apartment, he could pick his roommate
since he didn't have that luxury living in the dorm. When he
griped about living in the dorm, his parents made matters
worse by deciding it would be better if he had a roommate
rather than living on his own. They believed it would help
him get along with people better and keep him from being
reclusive the rest of his life.

As soon as he entered, he saw the mess that his roommate
had left in his wake. When he looked around the small
room, he wondered how people could live like this. Even
the dorm monitor had complained to Eric Hanson about his
lack of cleanliness. Since Eric moved here, they had had an
outbreak of gnats and sugar ants. He heard that his
roommate's parents were loaded. If this was true, Eric had
probably always had a maid to clean up after him and had
no idea how to pick up his own stuff.

As Royce dropped his books on his neatly made bed, he let
out a groan as he fully took in the disaster of their room.
The smell of sweaty socks and dirty clothes assaulted him.
He doubted any amount of room deodorizer would take
care of the rank smell in here. Feeling frustrated, he kicked

his roommate's belongings back to the other side of the room. How could one explain Eric living the way he did? No matter how many times he complained, the dude just shrugged his shoulders and did nothing.

Looking at the overflowing bed and a desk full of junk, he wondered how he got any studying done, much less sleep. Instead of cleaning off his bed, Eric had taken to sleeping on the floor with a pillow and a blanket that looked as if it hadn't been washed in years. It could probably stand up on its own and walk away. His desk was piled high with old food, garbage, and no telling what else. Eric's side of the dorm room could easily be a science experiment.

Once Royce had his side of the dorm free from Eric's mess, he settled down at his desk. His parents had complained that he was OCD, but after seeing how Eric lived, they now appreciated their son's mannerisms. That may be the only good thing that had come from living in this nightmare of a dorm.

As he turned on his computer, Eric burst through the dorm door. "Dude, did you hear about the carnival that set up near the college? It is going to be so cool. I'm gonna grab a couple of z's before heading over there tonight. It is going to be so righteous. They are only open at night and will be here for just a night or two. You have to go dude."

Royce shook his head, "I don't know. I have a lot of studying to do, and carnivals aren't my thing."

"Aw, come on. Don't be such a stick in the mud. Everyone is going."

Royce watched in disgust as Eric moved things around on the floor so he could take a nap. Deciding that hanging out at a carnival would be better than living in this filth for a few hours, he agreed, "You're right. I do need to get out of this room for a while."

***

The sounds of the carnival greeted them with a barrage of various noises, sights and smells. As the excitement of others around him became contagious, Royce thanked Eric for talking him into coming. This was just what he needed to forget about the slob of a roommate he had and his upcoming tests. After they had purchased their tickets, Royce looked around, trying to decide which ride he wanted to do first.

Everywhere he looked there were crowds of people and long lines as the masses moved about. He completely ignored the games; not wanting to waste his well earned money on them, and instead he headed straight to the rides. Heading over to them, an attraction caught his attention. The carnival had a Maze of the Tortured Fun House and a DarKastle Freak Show. He had never been to either and was curious to see what would be in the freak show. Maybe if he were lucky, it would be similar to the oddity museums his dad had taken him to over the years.

After the DarKastle Freak Show, another ride caught their attention. They followed the lights to the Bone Crusher Roller Ghoster. The bony grid of the roller coaster had a tiny string of cars that precariously perched at the summit of its first drop. The entrance to the ride was a large, maniacal clown face with fangs for teeth and red glowing eyes. The teeth looked as if they would chomp down on you at any moment.

***

Eric lost sight of Royce as the night progressed and figured that he would catch up with him at the dorm. The next morning he started to worry when Royce didn't make it home. That was not like his roommate; Royce was meticulous about his routines and would never skip a class.

By the time Eric reported Royce as missing, the carnival had long since moved on to another city. Royce had become one of the lost souls trapped for eternity in the carnival.

Chapter 15

The day after they departed the sleepy little towns, Joshua liked to see if there was anything in the news about any bodies being found or people being reported missing.

There on the front page of the local paper was a picture of the vice squad swarming a murder scene like a pack of wolves on the hunt. He shook his head in disgust; he didn't understand what had become of the human civilization anymore. It shamed him to even admit that at one time he had been mortal. This generation didn't appear to be very intelligent at all. Even those working in the law enforcement field seemed to walk around scratching their heads, trying to make the pieces fit together instead of actually using their minds to solve a case.

In the case of the recent murder victims, they could look as hard as they wanted, but they would never find the exact cause of death. They may discover the two small puncture wounds he left on the neck, but that would be all they found. He could have healed the neck wounds if he wished, but why should he do that? It was quite entertaining to watch as the stupid mortals tried to ascertain the cause of death. More times than not, they blamed a mysterious cult believing they were vampires; they never once believed that vampires existed. There had been times when it took a while for a body to be found. If it were discovered, all they could do was look at the dried up carcass and contemplate the cause of death.

As he surfed the web to find more information about any cases from their recent stops, he found one that was quite interesting. A news channel was running a live interview of some distraught parents in search of their missing daughter. A short, pudgy man was standing beside the parents. He must be the sheriff of the small town or one of the detectives working the case; either way, Joshua wasn't worried that they would discover any clues to her disappearance. If this guy represented this town's finest, he doubted that the cases would ever be solved.

Chapter 16

Oakdale, Mississippi
February, 2012

On the outskirts of this little town were The American Legion Hall and a large baseball field that was now abandoned. Those that had once belonged to the beloved charter here had passed away or had long since forgotten the importance of their meetings. The field was replaced with a larger, sleeker one near the local high school where more children could be encouraged to play.

This was the perfect place for the carnival to set up. The trees shivered in fear as the tractor trailers drove onto the ball field. It seemed as if the clouds fled, and the moon was desperate to hide from their presence tonight. Joshua stepped out of his truck and smelled the air. This sleepy little town of Oakdale, Mississippi was filled with souls ripe for the picking. They should be able to charge the games and fill the freezers with meat. Their stay in New Orleans would soon be here, and they had to ensure that they were prepared for the crowds. Once in New Orleans, they could fully recharge. While his power strengthened with each stop, he wanted more. He had grown tired of hiding in the night, keeping their existence unknown. It was time for the next stage of his plan. He had waited centuries for this; now, he was becoming impatient. This century was more open about zombies and vampires, anything that dealt with the supernatural. They wouldn't even realize what hit them when the time came.

A streak of lightning moved across the night sky, as though announcing their arrival to town. As a mist swirled around the field, the parade of travel trailers and eighteen wheelers formed a complete circle and were ready to be set up. The scene almost appeared to be an apparition in the sky as they hid in the shadows of the night. Smoke arose everywhere their feet touched the earth. Strange creatures took form, with skin that appeared to have a deathly white shade and long fangs protruded from their incisors. The animals of the night scurried away from the grotesque sight, fearing they would be on the menu for tonight's meal.

The sky opened up as the workers set up the big top tent, but they were used to working in the elements. All they cared about was setting up and opening the carnival so they could feed.

***

Jason Evans couldn't sleep. He was worried about his big test tomorrow. If he didn't pass, the coach would bench him because of his grades. He'd heard rumors that a professional scout would be in the crowd Saturday night to watch him play. This was his senior year of college, and he had high hopes of moving onto an NFL team. That would show the people in this small town that a man like him could make something of his life. Even though he had a scholarship, he barely made ends meet. He had shared an apartment with some fellow classmates, but his grades had slipped too badly. Which was one reason why he was in this current predicament. If he had kept his mind on his studies instead of partying, perhaps he wouldn't be worried about being benched.

Strange noises from outside caught his attention. He swore it was carnival music, but that couldn't be. He hadn't heard any mention of a carnival coming to town; nothing cool ever happened here.

He drew the curtains back and peered into the night. From his bedroom window, he thought he could see the top of a ferris wheel in the ball field that'd been abandoned for as long as he could remember.

Curious as to what was going on, he headed towards the field. As he got closer, a cold breeze from the direction of the carnival chilled him to the bone. He caught the scent of something in the air; it was an unpleasant odor, something unrecognizable. He could hear the sounds of a carnival flowing through the night. The calliope music sounded ominous to the level of almost threatening. It could put a spell on him if he listened to its eerie sound long enough.

He found some underbrush to hide in and watched as workers set up the rides and booths. It looked like there would be a roller coaster included in the rides along with a fun house. He bet this place would be full tomorrow with kids wanting to ride the rides, play the games, and sample food. Most of the kids here had never even seen a carnival before.

As he listened to the music, he felt a sense of something dark and unsettling about this place. From this distance, he would swear that the ferris wheel was made of human bone. He knew that it wasn't real bones, but this carnival definitely had a creepy factor to it. Some of the strict Baptist in this town would cause a ruckus about this carnival. They protested when the high school opened a haunted house for a fundraiser one year. They made the principal's life so miserable that year he decided not to bother with it the following year; instead, they elected to do a fall festival. That was a drag too because the kids at the school had a blast at the haunted house.

He watched in awe as bales of hay magically formed a makeshift fence around the carnival. He assumed the main attraction would be the big tent that had already been set up. It had definitely seen its better days as the canvas was stained and spattered with dark smears. A tall man walked out of the tent and stopped for a moment. He believed that he saw the man smell the air.

Jason jumped when he heard a voice behind him, "What brings you here tonight?"

He looked back at the tent and wondered how the man got here so fast without him noticing. "I was just curious as to what is going on."

The man rubbed his chin with his hand, "Hmm, well it's not opening night yet and we aren't prepared for any customers."

Something about him gave Jason the creeps. He didn't have the same build as him, but you could tell he was very muscular. His arms were covered in dark, disturbing looking tattoos, and he was dressed in all black.

"I'm sorry mister; I will leave. I don't want to make any trouble."

The man reached out and grabbed him with more strength than Jason would have suspected for a man his size, "I'm sorry son. You may not be looking for trouble, but I am looking for souls."

Jason shivered from the tone of the man's voice. He tried to free himself from his grasp, but it was too strong. He wasn't sure what the man meant by looking for souls, but he feared it wasn't good. The man continued, "How would you like to be made a permanent addition to this attraction?"

"No, that's okay mister. I have big dreams. I am going to be a famous football player and Saturday night is my chance to show everyone just how good I am."

He let out an evil laugh, "Well, unfortunately, you won't get that chance. You see we have our own way of dealing with Curious Georges."

He tried desperately to free himself from the maniacal grip of this creepy man. Suddenly, out of the shadows, more people appeared before him, all with glowing red eyes. He felt something warm run down his leg and realized he had peed on himself. He had never been more afraid in all of his life. Something told him that this would be his last day on this earth. When he saw the fangs, he knew that there really were things that went bump in the night.

His scream was drowned out by the wicked laughter from the vampires circling around him.

Chapter 17

Bigsby, North Carolina
April 2012

Debbie Harris pulled self-consciously at her clothes as she followed her friends out the door. Why in the world had she ever allowed Tara Jackson to pick out their clothes for the party tonight? She should have known that Tara would pick something that would embarrass her. She always secretly thought that Tara was jealous of her, and this outfit confirmed it. The clothes were at least one size too small and they showed off her body more than she liked. The whole reason she wore baggy clothes was so no one could tell what kind of figure she really had. After tonight, everyone would know.

She sure hoped that they at least had a good time without Tara being her normal self and upsetting everyone tonight. They were crashing the party as it was. This would be her first time to crash a party, much less a frat party. She heard that several of her classmates were going to be there. Brad Shipley's parents were away in Europe and he invited his friends to come over to his house for a party tonight. He had really spread the word so it should be a packed house. It was rumored that Brad was upset that his parents didn't take him to Europe and wanted to get back at them. He planned on letting everyone drink his dad's alcohol and take his mom's prescription drugs.

Tara swatted at Debbie's hands, "Stop that. People will look at you weird."

Debbie let out an exasperated sigh, "This outfit is uncomfortable."

"You look great and you will get used to it. You just need to relax and have a good time."

She scowled as they walked into the house. Some of the guys sitting outside made a low wolf call whistle in her direction. Trying to ignore them, she tucked a strand of hair nervously behind her ear.

As they pushed their way through another group of men, she diverted her gaze to the ground hoping to become invisible. She was becoming quite uncomfortable, and she had yet to enter the main part of the house. As they entered the living room where everyone seemed to be, she noticed cups of alcohol being passed around. As one made its way to her, she grabbed it and took a big gulp to help calm her nerves.

She looked around and saw that the rich, exquisite furniture had been carelessly placed along the walls of the room to give everyone space to dance. The room was larger than the great room at her house and was packed with dancing couples and friends out to have a good time. People were laughing and talking in raised voices in an attempt to be heard over the pounding music.

Debbie felt herself being dragged onto the dance floor and decided to lose herself in the music. The mood around her was contagious, and she began to relax. Soon, another drink found its way into her hands, and she gulped it down.

They had danced for almost an hour before she decided to go outside for some fresh air. Before heading out, she grabbed another drink to quench her thirst. As she made her way out the door, she caught a glimpse of Tara talking to two men.

Tara left her two companions and headed towards Debbie. She groaned when Tara asked, "You aren't leaving are you?"

Shaking her head, she replied, "No. I am just going outside for some fresh air." Suddenly she noticed how overwhelmingly hot and noisy the house was. Fresh air was just what she needed.

Leaving Tara to her two men, she walked out into the yard. There were several people scattered about the area, stumbling around and a few couples were making out under the trees.   She saw a wooden swing in the corner of the property that had wisteria growing up the trellis. This would be the perfect place to relax for a little while. She hurried over to the swing before someone else could claim it.

She swung ever so slightly and tilted her head back to admire the bright stars. She smiled softly as the alcohol she drank seeped further into her bloodstream. She could feel her insides warming from the effects of the booze.

***

This was the perfect place to come hunting for a snack. Everyone here was so drunk that he could merely sample and not kill anyone. No one would remember a thing. Actually, most would probably just pass out.

As he surveyed the crowd, someone handed him a drink. Walking around with the cup, he tried to blend into the crowd. The house was packed with drunk people; the party was in full swing as the music blared from the speakers. As he headed outside, he saw a girl sitting on a swing. She was wearing body hugging clothes that showed off her curves. Her legs were amazingly long and from this distance he could see her pulse beating in her neck. He felt a stirring deep inside of him as he gazed over her body. He watched as she unfastened her hair and let it cascade in thick waves down her back.

Her mouth was full, luscious and begging to be kissed. He watched as a young man headed her way, just like a moth to a flame. Not wanting to miss his chance, he beat the poor boy to the punch. He looked down at this gorgeous girl and couldn't decide if she should be a tasty morsel or to make her his. Something about her drew him to her.

He quietly asked, "Why are you out here all by yourself?"

She looked up at him with the greenest eyes he had ever seen and smiled seductively, "I just needed a bit of fresh air. It was getting warm in there."

He sat down beside her on the swing, "It does feel nice out here doesn't it? Are you having fun?"

"Oh, very much so. How about you?"

"I just got here, but I must say the night is sure looking good."

She smiled over at him. "Is that so?"

"How would you like to go for a walk away from all this noise?"

"I would rather dance a little more."

As they headed toward the dance floor, the music once again flowed through her. She could feel the music pulsing through the air, vibrating the floor of the house and hammering into her head. Now she wished she had agreed to go for a walk to somewhere peaceful and cool. As if reading her mind, he bent down, "Do you still want to dance?"

She looked around at the people having fun and looked back at this man who wanted to spend time with her. He had to be the most gorgeous man she had ever seen. When he smiled down at her, it was as if the music stopped playing and the room ceased to exist. He was the only thing she could see or feel. She nodded her head yes.

He took her hand in his and pulled her back outside. Her gaze traveled to his long, elegant fingers as his hand clasped hers firmly in his. As they walked down the street, her heart pounded in her chest. She looked up at him and managed another small smile. She found it amazing that he was interested in her. When he looked down at her, she swore she went into a trance. His eyes were mesmerizing; she had never seen eyes as dark as his. Her body reacted instantaneously to his very presence. For only a moment, she felt he was looking directly into her soul.

A shiver of desire climbed up her spine as she tried to stop the tempting thoughts from invading her mind. Now, she wished she had stayed on the dance floor. She wanted to feel those arms wrapped around her waist and holding her close to his body. She imagined what it would feel like to have her hands on his broad chest touching his thick muscles.

Desire was not something she had experienced before, but now as she walked in the dark with him, she knew she merely needed the right man to experience it with. She bit her lips as another shiver traveled through her body.

As if reading her thoughts, he stopped and turned her towards him. She took in every inch of his perfectly sculpted face. His eyes were as black as coal. Now and then she noticed a shimmer of something in the depths of them. It was almost as if there was an inner life inside of him glowing and drawing her in. His very being radiated a magnetism that captivated her. His eyelashes shadowed the planes of his chiseled cheekbones perfectly. No man could compete with him.

She longed to be with him more than she had ever wanted another man in her life. She wanted to pull those lips down to hers and kiss him. She imagined what they would feel like pressed to hers, kissing her with extreme passion.

Without even thinking about what she was doing, she raised her hands and placed them on his chest. She felt every detail of his rigid muscles beneath his tight black t-shirt. He stood well over six feet tall and towered over her short five foot three stature. She had to tilt her head back to look at him. His raven black hair fell just below his collar line. She wanted to run her fingers through his silky tresses.

He looked down at her with that penetrating gaze of his and drew her in even more. He asked in a deep husky voice that sent chills of pleasure up and down her spine, "What's your name?"

She swallowed hard, unsure if she could even find her voice. Trying to act demure, she playfully grinned up at him, "Debbie."

She wished she knew where this courage was coming from. She had never flirted with anyone before in her life and yet here she was flirting with this gorgeous man. Just one look from him set her body on fire.

He placed his hands on her hips and pulled her closer to him. She asked after a little hesitation, "What is your name?"

He whispered in her ear, "Joshua. Do you want to keep walking or do you want to go back?"

His voice sent shivers of desire down her body. His intense gaze caused her to lick her lips nervously, not wanting to share him with the other girls. She was unsure if she could trust herself alone with him either, "Where do you plan on going?"

He looked down at her, still unsure of his true intentions with this one, "We can walk. There is a park not too far from here. I want to get to know you better."

She stared at him with surprise in her eyes, unsure of why he wanted to get to know her more. Not trusting her voice one bit, she nodded in agreement. He bent his head down and lightly kissed her. That one touch sparked a desire in her very core and she knew at that moment she would walk to the ends of the earth with him.

He let himself read her mind and knew he intrigued her. This one would be easy to control and he found her interesting. One look into her eyes, and he saw the desire

she felt for him. If he turned her, he must remember what
her purpose would be. He must keep a distance from her.

As soon as his hands released her face, a sense of loss came
over her. She wished that contact hadn't been broken.

As they walked down the street towards the park, he looked
around to make sure no one was watching. Even though
the streets were packed with cars, no one paid them any
attention. He didn't bring anyone home until they started
to turn. It wouldn't do any good for them to get spooked
and run off knowing exactly where they came from. No,
this was easier. When they were still in the first stages of
being turned, it looked as if he was helping an inebriated
woman home from a night of too much partying.

When they reached the park, he pulled her down to sit next
to him on the bench. He placed his hands on her face and
drew her closer to him. The air crackled with electricity as
his thumb gently stroked her cheek.

She felt herself being drawn deeper into him. She became
completely lost as his magnetism drew her in. When she
saw his face bending down to her, she instinctively closed
her eyes. As soon as his lips touched hers, fireworks went
off deep inside of her.

She opened her mouth when she felt his tongue delve into
it. His hands entwined in her hair as he kissed her hungrily.
Her whole body turned to molten lava as she ran her fingers
through his wavy locks. She felt his firm body against hers
as she pulled him closer. His body's hard contours burned
into her flesh as an electrical charge of desire went straight
to the very center of her being. His hands glided over her
body leisurely and created havoc on her body with each

stroke. She was in a passion induced haze when he tilted her head back further, exposing her neck to him. She never felt his fangs pierce her tender skin. She unwittingly gave herself to him completely. He had never had one desire him so readily as this young imp. She would be a pleasure to have in his family.

***

Debbie heard the words coming out of Joshua's mouth, but her mind refused to believe what he was saying. *Vampire.* That one word was enough to send a cold chill of terror down her spine. She tried to swallow back the fear rising up inside of her throat, but it was too dry. Her lips were chapped and starting to crack. She couldn't even muster up enough moisture to bring some relief to them. She couldn't remember the last time she'd had anything to drink. Her insides felt as if they were on fire.

She would give anything for just a drop of water right now. She was miserable, and this man whom she had found sexy was spouting off nonsense about turning her into a vampire. Something told her death would have been far better than what he had in store for her. She had never been able to take the sight of blood. Just one look at a drop of it and she passed out cold.

Chapter 18

Julius Williams looked back at the parking lot. He hoped no one complained about the missing person flyers he had blanketed the windshields with. After all, he was searching for his sister and not selling anything. This was the last night that the carnival would be here and he had a hard time finding out where they would be going next. It seemed as if he was always a day behind them, but this time he somehow managed to catch up, but by tomorrow, they would probably be gone.

Since he still had a few flyers left, he planned on handing them out inside the carnival hoping someone had seen her. As he left the parking lot, he heard someone holler, "You there. What are you doing?"

Julius whirled around to see a burly man headed his way. His eyes were clearly blazing with anger, Julius stammered, "I..I... I am putting out these flyers. My sister is missing."

He handed a flyer to the man. Instead of taking it, the man folded his arms close to his chest and leered at him. There was something unsettling about this big man. Without warning, he snatched the flyer from Julius's hand. "Nope, I haven't seen her."

Julius wasn't sure what to say. There was no way the man had a good look at the flyer. He swung his arm over to the entrance and pointed, "This is our last night here. You are more than welcome to go look around. I doubt that you will find her though. I would have seen her if she had come to the carnival.”

“She has been missing for a while now, but thank you. I would like to look around. Maybe someone who works here will remember seeing her.”

The man shrugged his shoulders, “You can see, but I doubt it. The workers here see hundreds of faces day in and day out. But go ahead and ask around.”

A shiver went through Julius as the guy ushered him to the entrance. For a moment, he thought the man’s eyes gleamed in the moonlight. As they neared the entrance, Julius noticed just how eerie the music was. There was something dark and ominous about the whole carnival. Even the workers were dressed gloomily.

Even though it was almost midnight, the lines were still long. The rides lit up the night sky.

The large man told Julius, “Go on and walk around. You are more than welcome to talk to the workers, but I don’t think they can help you.”

As he shook the man’s hand, he noticed how cold it was, “Thank you so much all the same.”

Before he could say anything further, the man left. As he made his way through the crowd of people, he paid special attention to the young girls, hoping that he would find his sister. The music was so loud that it vibrated his bones. He never expected it to be like this.

He saw the carousel and for some unknown reason he felt drawn to it. The closer he walked to it, a sense of helplessness became oppressive. He fought hard to overcome it. The longer he stared at the horses he began to notice their monstrous faces. The center of the ride was a large mirrored cylinder. There was something hypnotic about watching the carousel go round and round. The reflections of the riders turned grotesque looking. As if in a trance, he just stared at the reflections. In the next instant, he jumped back. He swore one of the distorted images just tried to jump out at him. It scared him so bad that he nearly peed in his pants. He blinked several times as he stared at the mirror waiting to see if it happened again, but nothing did.

As he staggered away from the carousel, it took a while for everything to come into focus once more. He stared back at the carousel to see if any more figures tried to jump out from the mirror when he bumped into something. It was a game made to test your strength. The long pole resembled a bone with a bell attached to the top and a pad at the bottom that you hit with a sledge hammer.

He continued to wander the carnival, but found himself drawn more to the game booths. There were rows and rows of vendors with different games. Several of the announcers were talking all at once, "Come win a prize, try your luck, four throws for a dollar, and win your girl a prize." There was a ring toss, a strange game where you shot down creepy looking black cats, and his favorite game, skeeball. There was one game that seemed to draw in the crowds; it had clear glass bowls, dishes, vases, and cups that you threw a coin inside. The glassware shined in the lights as if they were magical, which could be why the game was so popular. If your coin landed in the object, you kept whatever was in it. The only catch was you had to supply the coins. He saw moms rifling through their purses and dad's digging in their pockets in search of coins.

Seeing the moms with their children made him realize just how much his mom must miss his sister. His mom was close to both of them, but Amber was the baby and still at home.

Maybe, he should give her a call tonight, just to touch base and see how she was doing. He dreaded calling her. She always asked if he had found out anything and every time he had to break her heart.

As he watched the operator work the booth, he noticed that she took the goth look a little too far and was extremely pale. It wouldn't hurt her to get out in the sun for a little while. The bright red lipstick didn't help her complexion. It seemed to wash her out even more. Her long black hair was highlighted with blood red streaks as well. She was dressed in form fitting black clothes that showed off what little curves she had.

A breeze blew through the carnival carrying with it a foul odor, almost as if something was decaying nearby. He wrinkled his nose at the smell and looked around to see if he could find the source.

The young girl manning the game booth noticed his displeasure and sauntered up to him, "Wanna try your luck at the game mister?"

He shook his head, "No, that's okay. I am looking for my sister." He handed her the flyer, "She was last seen at this carnival before she disappeared."

She studied the flyer and handed it back to him, "I'm sorry mister; she doesn't look familiar, but I see so many faces."

He looked at her one more time as she handed him back the flyer and noticed just how dark her eyes were. They were black as coal, and you couldn't see any color in the irises.

The young girl told him, "Make sure you stop by the hamburger cart. Everyone loves our burgers. They say they are the best they've ever had."

He nodded his head, but he knew after smelling the foulness in the air, he wouldn't be eating here, "Yeah okay. Thanks."

As he walked away, he smelled it again. If possible, it smelled worse than before. He looked around to see if he could figure out where it was coming from.

After walking around aimlessly for a few minutes, he found himself standing in front of the fun house. It was as if his sister was calling him in there. The number of people inside was oppressive. As soon as he walked in, he felt claustrophobic, hot, and hemmed in. The odor in here was just as bad as outside. He wasn't sure if it was body odor or something even more foul. As bad as he wanted to leave, he found himself being pulled in deeper.

It consisted of a series of walkways with an assortment of mirrors that distorted your image. Sporadically placed around were several wax figures. He was curious to know how they kept them from melting from the heat in here. One particular figure that he found unnatural was a clown dressed in black with glowing red eyes, but instead of a smile, it had a sneer with sharpened teeth. He had no desire to meet that creature in a dark alley. There were skulls and crossbones displayed along the walls along with bats and spider webs hanging from the ceiling. He thought that the music playing in the carnival was creepy, but the music in here was downright ghastly.

The group of boys in front of him was complaining about how lame they found the place. He had to agree. What drew most of the younger crowd here was the mirror covered walls that distorted your features.

One section was decorated with vampires. One even hung down from the ceiling, and it appeared to be feeding off of a live victim. Just looking at it caused him to shudder. He looked at the mirror placed right by the prop and was amazed at how lifelike it appeared. He wondered how they managed this since the prop's reflection did not show in the mirror. In the movies he had seen the vampire's reflection never appeared in a mirror. Maybe it was sprayed with a non-reflective silver paint. Intrigued, he stepped in front of the mirror and was surprised to see his reflection. When he went out to touch it, someone behind him pushed him forward.

As he walked out of the fun house, he heard a voice on the loudspeaker announce that the carnival was closing and thank everyone for coming. He walked out of the carnival disappointed that he didn't find any clues to the whereabouts of his sister.

***

Joshua watched as the crowd left, and the lights went out. The carnies gathered around him. He called out to his shape shifters, "It is time to leave. We had a man here looking for his sister. I want to dismantle and leave before he goes to the local police. We did good while we were here, but it is time to move on."

The wolves took the shape of humans and quickly picked up the area. They knew that the carnies would go to bed without bothering to assist.

Joshua walked over to the carousel as a menacing grin formed on his face. He watched in glee as the souls pounded on the mirror, trying to free themselves from their prison. They'd gathered a few more tonight. With each soul they trapped, they increased the power of the carnival, and he'd collected a few for his personal use.

He remembered being first turned and how hard it had been eating. He never thought of stealing a soul back then. Even now, most vampires didn't realize they could steal souls to become stronger. The carnival had been his best idea since it made collecting souls so much easier. It was a great way to lure food to them without having to go out into the public.

These mortals were easily enticed with lights, rides, and games. It had always been that way. A carnival made parents feel safe when leaving their child with a stranger. He let out a silent chuckle, *"If they only knew the truth."* His carnival was one of the most dangerous places on this earth, especially for the living.

Since the carnies were still shrouded in darkness, they let their true forms take shape. Some were still hungry and wanted to go find a bite to eat before going to sleep.

Chapter 19

Baton Rouge, Louisiana
March 2013

Shortly before midnight, with a full moon hanging high in the sky, the carnival workers loaded up and prepared to head out into the night. As the eighteen wheelers brought them to their next destination, they waited for what was yet to come.

Several trucks, camper trailers, motor homes, and other vehicles made up the parade of rides and games that made their way to New Orleans, Louisiana for the Mardi Gras festivities. They were always in New Orleans for Mardi Gras; it was their busiest time of the year.

When they arrived in New Orleans, it would be daybreak so they would rest and set up in the middle of the night. They needed to sleep as the next few nights would be extremely busy.

As soon as they arrived at their destination, the vehicles arranged themselves in a rough circle around the perimeter of the field. They were almost on the outskirts of the city, but that did not matter. Parents and kids would still flock to them. Once the last truck parked, they cut off the engines and were swallowed by the quietness of the night. The only noise that filled the air was the buzz from the generators. All were tucked into their beds.

If you headed closer to New Orleans, you could hear the sounds of this great city. From where they were, you had to strain to hear the music that pulsed throughout the city. However, for them to have enough room for their carnival, they needed the extra space, and this was the only place they could find.

New Orleans was truly a city that never slept, which might be why they did so well here. They fit in with the nightlife. They would stay longer than their usual time if they could figure a way to make it work; unfortunately, the reason they were so successful was they never stayed in the same place for long. New Orleans was the only place that remained a constant in their routine. Other than here, they found little towns to set up and run for two nights before moving on. With the promise of a heavy portion of the sales going to the city, they had never been denied.

As they woke up the following night, a wispy stream of fog swirled and snaked through the area. As the night sky grew darker, it became more opaque and grew heavier. Shapes, featureless at first, took form in the fog becoming more recognizable as the hours wore on. The shapes drifted about the field. The outlines became more identifiable as their size and definition improved. The tent took shape as the big top went up and other squares and rectangles became concession stands and game booths. The heavy mist clung to everything. Suddenly, a blast of light filled the night air as the carnival came to life. Soon, it would be teaming with customers wanting to enjoy the shows and take turns on the rides. The night air would be filled with the smell of cotton candy, hot dogs, chili, and funnel cakes being fried.

***

Claire St. Martin passed under a neon sign that shined bright against the dark sky and groaned when she heard the annoying buzz. Ignoring the sign, and the men going into the bar, she continued to strut down the street. Her hips swayed back and forth rhythmically as her high heels clacked on the sidewalk. Her miniskirt and top left nothing to the imagination, and the black fishnet stockings fit her legs like a second skin. She passed by the window of a video store announcing that they were closing their doors forever. The next store's window had lights arranged to highlight local art. She caught her reflection as she walked by but paid no attention. She didn't have to; she knew she was dressed perfectly for the job.

From behind her, the low rumble of a car caught her attention as its headlights lit up the street in front of her. The beams, a welcomed coincidence, landed on her derriere to show off how shapely and inviting it was.

She slyly glanced over her shoulder and saw that it was a brand new Mercedes. She licked her lips both in anticipation and to entice to the driver.

The Mercedes passed her without slowing. She wasn't worried though. She knew exactly how this pas de deaux played out. The car would make the block and head back towards her; they always did.

***

He smirked to himself as he followed the woman. He blended in with the darkness of the night. His stealth movements were planned and precise just like a wolf stalking its prey.

All of a sudden, the dark clouds parted to reveal a full moon. As rapidly as the clouds parted, they covered the moon once again. A satisfied smile formed on her face as the Mercedes pulled up next to her. The tinted window slid down to reveal a slightly overweight, balding man sitting in the driver's seat. The dark figure ducked into the alleyway, waiting to see what happened next.

***

She leaned down on the car and pushed a lock of her hair behind her ear. She was practically falling out of her halter top shirt. "Looking for a little excitement tonight cher," she asked in a sweet yet a seductive tone.

"You offering?" He coyly asked.

She smiled, "You got the money?"

When he waved a handful of bills in front of her, she stood up tall and sashayed a few steps away from the car. She felt the man's eyes following her every move.

She looked back over her shoulders and beckoned him with a come hither glance. She confidently strode to the edge of the building that led to the alleyway. An alcove in the back was perfect for what she had in mind.

The man shut off the engine and stepped out of the car. Enticing him to follow her, she inched up her skirt and moved her hands suggestively up and down her thigh.

"Wouldn't you rather do this in the car?"

She let out a sultry laugh, "I have a warm place for you. Don't you worry now."

She took the man's hand and led him to the alcove.

A noise towards the back of the alley caught their attention. Several thoughts ran through each of their minds. A mangy cat darted from behind a dumpster and the man laughed. She breathed a sigh of relief; she had feared that maybe a cop had stumbled upon them. "That stupid cat scared me half to death."

A figure suddenly emerged from the darkness.

***

He stared at the two of them wondering which he would feast on first. He grabbed the woman by the neck with one hand and the man with the other. He lifted the woman off the ground as her legs and arms flailed; he quickly drained the man dry. He looked at the woman and planned on savoring the experience with her.

Chapter 20

New Orleans, Louisiana
March 2013

When he heard the sound of the stilettos on the sidewalk, he instinctively ducked into the shadows of the alleyway. He had always been careful to stay out of view when hunting for food away from the carnival. Whenever anything bad happened in a town where a carnival visited, locals tended to blame the carnies; although, this time it would be true. Still, he didn't want any extra attention brought to the carnival at this time.

He purposefully dressed in black. It allowed him the ability to meld into the darkness of the night and made him virtually invisible. This was a predatory skill he had mastered almost a century ago.

Even in the darkness, he saw his prey. His night vision was better than most like him. Since he had spent most of his life in dark, confined spaces, this was a much-needed trait.

***

Stacie Allen had always been a looker and used those looks to her advantage. Unlike others in her profession, she prided herself on being a high priced jezebel. Right now, she was late for one of her "dates". If she didn't hurry, he was liable to go looking for someone on the street. Usually, she was early, but today had not played out well at all.

Whenever she passed in front of a man, her appearance made them look twice. Her raven black hair was so dark, sometimes it had a blue hue to it. Her eyes were a steel gray with flecks of blue. Her dates had commented that they could get lost in her eyes just by watching them change colors with the increase of her passion.

The night air caressed her skin as she tried to beat the rain. For a moment, she thought she heard something behind her and stopped to glance backwards. Her eyes peered through the darkness, but she saw nothing to concern her. The streets were quiet tonight. Most people wanted to avoid the potential downpour that threatened to come down at any moment. She picked up her pace and walked into the fog that snaked through the streets. Suddenly, a figure appeared ahead of her and seemed to be headed straight for her. Her breath caught for a moment as it started to drizzle. Not bothering to approach the man, she slipped off her shoes and hurried along.

She saw the cemetery up ahead and decided to cut through it to save her some time. She passed through the wrought iron gates and followed the path that led her through the whitewashed tombs that eerily stood out against the blackness of the night.

***

As he followed his prey, he couldn't help but feel powerful. Walking freely among these humans made him feel superior to them; it reminded him that he was truly invincible. For years, he'd found his food among these imbecile humans without ever being detected. It sent a rush through him knowing that he could stand here in the shadows, and no one would know what he had been doing right under their noses. However, it was time to make his presence known. Until now, no one had a clue as to their identity. They walked these same streets without one single person knowing or even suspecting that vampires existed. He had felt untouchable all these years and was ready to show just how cunning he actually was.

He savored the memories of his kills. What he enjoyed most of all though was collecting the victims' souls. He found it satisfying to know those souls were contained in the confines of the carnival. When he had started the carnival, it was for this very purpose. There was a compulsion deep inside of him to trap these souls here with him. He pinned her to the ground, but as soon as he looked into her eyes, time seemed to stand still. Everything around him vanished. For once the world around him became quiet; he no longer smelled the offensive smell of human food, and all he smelled was the blood pumping through her body. Nothing else mattered to him at this moment other than this mere woman. Fate had brought them together.

His gaze traveled over her body, and he instinctively wanted to possess every part of her. Every fiber of his being wanted to sweep her away from this world and keep her all to himself, regardless if she was willing or not.

Before she could scream or react, his teeth sank into the delicate skin of her neck. A crimson ribbon of blood flowed from the two puncture wounds on her neck. He took her into his arms and raised her ever so slightly. Her raven black tendrils spilled across the hands he placed behind her head. Unable to resist her luscious lips, he kissed her. Desire shot through her body like an electrical current from his very touch. His lips left hers as they traveled down her neck, finding once again the wound he'd created. His sensuous mouth encircled the wound and greedily drank from her.

A scarlet necklace formed across her delicate collarbone, reminiscent to tiny rubies against her skin. He licked each morsel passionately, savoring her sweet blood. He felt her writhe against him.

As he turned his victim, he knew that she was more than food; she would be perfect to lure men into his family. While unconscious from the shock of being bitten, he carried her off into the night. He knew from experience that the victim of a vampire bite would only remember the feeling of pure ecstasy and never the actual bite. If it were just that they needed to be fed, he wouldn't worry with killing those he fed on. However, he needed their souls for his power. He had done this all in secret. Soon it would be their time, they would be the dominant race and these mortals would be nothing more than food for their survival.

As they approached the carnival, he beamed with pride. From here, it looked completely dark and ominous; just how he wanted it. No one outside of his carefully chosen family knew of its mysteries, and he planned to keep it that way.

***

As Stacie slowly regained consciousness, she saw him standing over her, "It's about time you awoke. There is much we need to discuss. What I am about to tell you may sound outlandish and bizarre, but it will be the truth."

She blinked and swallowed back the fear. She slowly nodded, fearing what this man might do. Was he planning on killing her and wanted to explain the reasoning behind it before doing so?

Slowly, he informed her, "I am a vampire. As soon as I saw you, I knew you were more than food and that you must join my family."

She knew that New Orleans was full of motier foux, crazies, but so far, this was the first one she had ever encountered. She responded, "Vampires aren't real. They are just a fairy tale someone made up to scare little children."

He let out a harsh laugh, "Oh my dear, vampires are real and soon you will find out just how real we are. I have plans for you my lovely one. With your stunning good looks, you will do better than my other female charges."

She let out a laugh, "You are demented. There is no such thing as vampires, I tell you."

She heard him tsking her, "But you see there is. Years ago we ruled the land, but the High Council felt that we shouldn't use humans as our primary food source. As the raiding of villages stopped and time moved on, the public soon forgot about the slaughtering of innocent lives by vampires. The foolish mortals let their guard down, and now we go into the world unheeded. Trust me my dear; we are more than myths created to scare innocent little children."

She looked at him and wondered if she could really be talking to a vampire or if this guy had a screw or two loose. She shook her head, trying to clear the heavy fog that clouded her mind.

He told her, "It has taken me centuries to find one such as you; one who could help lure men into my family. I have a few, but none actually meet my criteria for what I plan to do. With you, I may be able to reach my dreams."

In the next instant, she realized something was terribly wrong with her. The room violently spun and her body shook uncontrollably. She had a hard time breathing and felt ill to her stomach. She asked, "What is wrong with me?"

He replied, "You are going through the transformation stage. It only lasts a short time. Remember to breath and let the change take its course."

Tears rolled down her cheeks as the pain consumed her body, "Please make it stop. It hurts too bad!" She swore her body was being liquefied from the inside out. When she didn't think she could take any more, the pain suddenly subsided. All that remained was a dull ache in the back of her head.

She asked, "What is happening to me?"

He replied, "The transformation stage is almost complete. Not too long from now, you will have an insatiable hunger for blood, and possibly flesh, take over your body. It won't be too much longer before you are completely turned into a vampire."

Just the idea of drinking human blood turned her stomach. This had to be a nightmare.

Chapter 21

The silk felt good against Josie's flesh as she slipped it off her shoulders. She walked over to the mirror and wished she could see her reflection, but she hadn't seen that reflection in decades now. Some men preferred the milky white look of her skin, but she wished she could feel the sun against it once more.

She ran her hands down her firm and supple body. If only she had been given a chance to see what she would have looked like as a full-grown woman, but her life had been cut short at such a young age of barely nineteen.

She ran her tongue down her elongated incisors as she looked at the young boy lying on her bed. Joshua had sent him to her trailer as a treat. She wondered if he knew what she was doing. He often asked her how many souls she captured that night. She had become quite good at lying to him; now she could look him straight in the eyes and lie. She had also become efficient at keeping him from intruding on her thoughts. She taught Tyler the same trick so when they were together, no one, not even other members of the family, could intrude on their thoughts.

Looking down at this boy, she knew she couldn't end his life. He was simply too young. He needed a chance to grow up and savor life. If she turned him, he would eventually hate her just as she hated her maker.

As she walked away from the bed, she was aware of the suppleness and tone of her body. Her legs were taut and her abdomen flat. Her upper arms were well defined; the outline of her biceps clearly evident.

How long had it been since she was turned? She had lost count over the years. Could it be almost a century now? She shook her head. Surely it wasn't that long ago. She had been so young when Joshua asked her to follow him, and his offer sounded so tempting.

She crawled into her hidden compartment in the trailer and welcomed the sleep that had been enticing her in the early morning hours. Hopefully by the time daylight came, the young man would have left. As she settled into sleep, she let out a soft sigh. If only she could close her eyes and not recall the lives she had taken over the years. She eventually succumbed to a restless slumber.

When she woke up, the young man was indeed gone. Maybe Tyler had found him and sent him on his way. Hunger quickly took over her body. If she didn't feed tonight, she wouldn't be able to control it. She stepped into her costume, a black leather bustier with a pair of tight leather pants. The bustier was designed to show off her body to its best potential, and it accentuated the milkiness of her alabaster skin.

As she walked to her game booth for the night, she saw a commotion near the entrance. A young man was giving a group of girls a hard time. She could tell instantly that this one was trouble. He would be perfect for her breakfast. She had no problems with feeding off of those that were already tortured souls. She had learned how to read minds to find those that came to the carnival to lure young children away for their own sick and twisted appetites. She didn't mind condemning their souls to hell for eternity; they deserved to be tortured. It was the innocent ones that she had a hard time feeding on.

She would make sure that she caught his eye and lured him to her booth. Looking over at him, she noticed that he had the barest hint of a mustache and a scar just above his right eye. From what she could tell, his arms were covered in tattoos and one snaked around his neck.

As she manned her booth, she saw Joshua walk to the entrance to open the carnival. There was a boldness that death had not taken away from his features. He strived to keep his body fit. Her eyes roamed over his body and took in its sheer perfection. The outline of his pectorals was clearly evident through his black t-shirt. His muscles rippled with his every move. His tight black jeans hugged his body sinfully. She also knew what lurked beneath his sinful exterior.

Her eyes broke away from Joshua when her breakfast prospect appeared at her booth, "I saw you looking at me earlier babe. I can give you a better time than that one there, I promise."

She smiled at him, "I am sure you can. I get off in an hour. Why don't you meet me at my trailer and show me just how good of a time you can give me?"

"Sure babe. Just tell me where."

As he played the game, she gave him directions to her trailer. When he flexed his arm to throw the baseball at the target, she noticed the fullness of the veins that ran through his arm. They seduced her; calling her to him. She couldn't wait to get him alone. She could already taste his blood.

At closing time, she hastily closed her game booth and walked briskly over to her trailer. She wanted to feed before Tyler returned to the trailer. When she opened the door, she saw her breakfast sprawled out on the bed. Looking into his eyes, she saw his life dance in his irises. He pulled her down to the bed and kissed her. The warmth of his body against her cold flesh was an aphrodisiac. She felt his heart pumping hard against his chest. The steady throb reverberated throughout her body. She could hear the blood pulsing through his veins; its sound was music to her ears. She pressed her face deep into the crook of his neck and ran her tongue along the sweet spot she was about to penetrate. She suddenly bit hard into his flesh, savoring the sweet taste of him.

After she had finished feeding, she disposed of the body. It would soon be daylight, but she was still restless. Woefully, she crawled into her bed and hoped that since she was full that sleep would come quickly. She tossed and turned fitfully until she finally fell asleep. That was when the dreams came.

She woke up suddenly covered in a cold sweat. It took her a moment to realize she was still in her room and that it was only a dream, but it felt so much more than that. She kept reliving the day she was made; the day she was cursed to walk among the dead for eternity craving blood. She had thought working for the carnival and being around those like her would help calm her but it hadn't. The dreams had become worse lately; they were more like nightmares actually.

She feared more and more innocent lives were being taken. That was something she had difficulty dealing with. She had been keeping her thoughts well guarded, so others didn't read her mind, but lately, she had considered reaching out for help and ending this charade. What they were doing was wrong, and she had to put a stop to it, but how?

As she got up, she shook her head to clear her mind of the foggy memories and her tortured thoughts. Regardless of how she felt, she still needed to work tonight. She also needed to guard her thoughts, or it meant a painful death for her.

She stepped into the shower and scrubbed her body vigorously hoping to bring a little color to her skin if even for only a short while. She had grown accustomed to feeding off of others, but it was watching those that she cared about growing old and die that she despised while she never aged. Of course, she had to watch those she cared about from afar; she could never let them know that she still walked this earth. As far as they knew, she died decades ago. All that remained of her family was a long lost relative; someone too frail and old now. Her parents died too many years ago. She had visited the funeral home in the early morning hours to say goodbye to them. She slowly fingered her mother's pendant that she had taken from her as she recalled her happy childhood. If only she could go back and change things. She would do things so differently. Now, she realized that the rules they implemented were not because they didn't love her or to make her life miserable, but instead, they were to keep her safe and out of harm's way. She learned that the hard way and now, she must suffer the consequences.

Chapter 22

New Orleans, Louisiana
March 2013

The pink and orange hues of sunrise held the promise of another day. Ashley stood on the edge of the riverbank watching as the sun rose over the mighty Mississippi River. She waited in anticipation for the sun to rise because she couldn't remember the last time she'd seen an actual sunrise. She looked up to the sky and watched as the various colors melded together. She nervously ran her hands through her hair, contemplating her decision once again.

Ever since being turned, she had despised this new life. When Joshua found her at that diner, she honestly believed that her life had taken a turn for the better. Now, she was unsure of what he was doing. She could no longer live with herself and do his bidding. These were innocent lives he was taking; he was not doing it for food, but for power. He always warned them about feeding on too many humans in any one town, but she wondered if he practiced what he preached.

Since she had no one to confide in about her fears, she decided it was time for her life to end. To her, it was the only logical conclusion to her dilemma. She would no longer have to feast on human flesh and no longer have to trap poor souls into the confines of the carnival.

Earlier, she had slipped away without anyone's knowledge. She knew it was time to end this charade. The carnival would soon leave New Orleans, and she could not bear to continue on with them.

As the sun rose over the river, she realized just how much she had missed the sunshine kissing her skin during the day. She couldn't remember how long it had been since she'd welcomed a new day by watching a sunrise and not a sunset. She would no longer be forced into darkness as the sun rose. It was strange how at peace she was with her decision.

As the orange globe rose higher in the sky, her instinct to survive kicked in and she had to resist the urge to run from its harmful rays. It didn't take long for the ultraviolet rays from the sun to begin to take effect on her skin. It started out as a mere tingling sensation that soon turned to itching. The itching turned into a burning pain as the sun's rays ate away at her skin. As the sunlight washed over her body, an idea took form in her head, but for this plan to work, she had to be alive.

With the speed no mere mortal would ever have, she propelled her body back to her sanctuary. By the time she arrived back at the carnival, an intense pain had consumed her whole body. She had to choke back a scream as to not wake anyone.

She slipped into her dark confines and appreciated the cool darkness of her coffin. Pain coursed through her body, causing her to gasp in short breaths of air as her skin sizzled; the burns covering her body continued to blister. She needed fresh blood to rejuvenate herself, or her body would never begin the healing process. For once, she was thankful she kept a stash of blood hidden in her trailer. At first, she felt guilty about deceiving her family, but now this may be what saved her miserable life. Easing herself from her coffin, she opened the hidden compartment and pulled out a bag of O+ blood. Fresh would be better, but this would have to do for now. It was the freshest she had; she'd purchased it a night or two ago. She learned quickly after being turned that there was a black market for blood, but it was typically used for those mere mortals who wished to be vampires and wanted to drink human blood.

She pulled the cap off and squeezed the cold blood into her mouth, drinking hungrily. She quickly drained three bags of blood before finally feeling satisfied.

She tucked herself back into her coffin and fell fast asleep while her body rapidly healed itself. She may not ever conquer the thirst she had for human blood, but for now she could help humanity. She would do her best to stop what was going on here. She had to help these humans from falling prey to these vampires. The trick would be keeping the humans from being slaughtered, but also hide the fact that she was saving these humans from the very vampires she had called friends.

Chapter 23

New Orleans, Louisiana
March 2013

As soon as Guy Mayon pulled up to his office, he let out a groan. In front of his entrance was a man pacing back and forth. Instinctively, he knew that this was a new client. They all had the same forlorn look and you could see the desperation in their eyes. What had made it worse was the release of the news story about his success in finding missing family members; people from all over had been reaching out to him for help. His buddy, former Detective Mike Bailey with the New Orleans Police Department, left the bureaucracy and politics behind and came to work with him.

After seeing how far the corruption went in the police department and various political offices around here, Mike didn't need much convincing. Guy was about to call Mike when he drove up. Guy preferred they both meet with potential clients together, that way they didn't have to rehash everything again. Besides, Mike had great instincts and together they tended to ask a range of questions that made it easier in locating those that simply ran away from home.

They both walked up to the door at the same time. The man stopped pacing and extended his hand out to Guy first, "My name is Julius Williams. I have a problem that I believe you can help me with. I have read about you in the paper Mr. Mayon and you may be my only chance."

Guy shook his hand and introduced Mike, "This is my partner Mike Bailey. Until recently, he worked with the New Orleans Police Department."

Julius shook his head, "Yes, I read about you in the paper. You were brave to take on the mob here in New Orleans. You two may be my only hope."

As Guy unlocked the office door and ushered them inside, he asked, "How can we help you?"

"My sister went missing over six months ago. The local authorities believe that she ran away, but that is not like Amber. She wanted to leave town, but she had always stuck to her guns that after she had graduated she was leaving. She was only a few months away from graduating. Her grades were good, so she wasn't trying to hide something. My parents are beside themselves with worry."

Mike asked, "What led you here Mr. Williams?"

"My sister was last seen at a carnival. I checked with the town officials, and they verified that the carnival company did ask for permission to set up. They also requested that everything be kept quiet for intrigue. I have tried following the carnival, but they don't advertise where they are going to next so it has been hard. I did some research on this particular carnival. New Orleans is the only city they ever visit more than once and only during Mardi Gras. I also checked into missing person's reports and wherever they go a missing person's report was filed soon after."

That piqued Guy's curiosity, "Are you certain about that? If that is the case, then the authorities should have noticed a pattern."

"As I said, there isn't much information on the carnival and they never announce where they are going. It took me a while to put two and two together. I was going through a missing persons' database and noticed a number of people that were last seen at a carnival just like my sister. That has to be more than a coincidence."

Mike asked, "And you are sure that this carnival is the same one that your sister went to?"

He nodded his head, "Yes, her friend Chris had taken pictures that night. I was hoping to show them around there again tonight. One of the workers has to remember something."

Guy exclaimed, "Let's not ask around at the carnival just yet. If someone there is involved in these disappearances, we don't want to let them know we are onto them. If they are holding these missing persons captive and we tip our hat, there is a chance they will kill them."

Julius handed them the photos, "So then you will help me?"

Guy replied, "I can't promise you anything right now, but I will look into it. I would rather you let us ask the questions before going to the carnival yourself."

Mike asked, "Where exactly did you say the carnival was?"

"It is near the edge of town; it looks as if it is on an abandoned car lot."

Mike shook his head, "It could be. After Hurricane Katrina hit, a lot of area businesses have not been rebuilt."

Mike looked over at his friend, "Well, mon ami, when was the last time you went to the carnival?"

Guy scratched his head as he thought about that, "Mais, I was probably a teenager, if that. My parents took us to the state fair every year until they decided we were too old for it. But, then again, they may have been tired of dealing with the people and lines. My dad despised big crowds and wasting money. When you go to one of those things, you spend money for every little thing, and he didn't like that one bit. He preferred to take us to Mardi Gras parades every year because we could have a blast without it costing him a dime. We came back home with bags full of doubloons, beads, and all kinds of other things. If he didn't have to spend money, he didn't mind the crowds. We got there early in the morning and found a good spot to watch the parade. He had already found out the parade route, and we sat towards the end. He knew that the floats would want to unload anything left on them at the end of the route and as they passed by, they just started dumping. We always lucked out with lots of loot."

Mike realized that if there were any credence to what this guy had told them, then this case would be extremely interesting. Even Mike couldn't remember the last time he had been to a carnival, but he was ready to go and do some snooping. He first planned on researching this carnival to see if he could learn more about any missing persons' reports that may have been made where the carnival visited.

Julius hesitated before informing the both of them, "I don't know how much you charge, but I don't have a lot of money. I will gladly pay you for an hour or two of your time. I had to take time off from work, and I have spent most of my savings chasing down this carnival. I hate to return home empty handed, but this is my last chance."

Guy told him, "Let's worry about price after we look into this some. I don't want to take your money if this isn't something we can help you with."

Mike broke in, "I want to look into the missing persons' reports before we even head over to the carnival. Please leave your sister's picture with us so that we can have it handy when we go to the carnival. I also want to have a few photos of the other missing persons in case we find them there. Someone may have decided that the carnival life was for them and ran away from home."

As Julius handed over the pictures he had of his sister, he replied, "That just doesn't sound like Amber."

As Mike looked at the pictures of Amber, he said, "No, but maybe we can find another missing person while there. You never know; maybe, someone will remember your sister. Sometimes they are afraid of talking to the local police, but since this happened in another state, and we aren't the police, they may open up to us more."

Guy asked, "Is there a number we can reach you at in case we do find out anything?"

Julius jotted down his phone number, "It's expensive to stay in hotels, so I am camping right now. You can reach me on my cell phone."

Mike felt sorry for the man. He sure hoped that Julius hadn't been chasing a dead lead as far as the carnival went.

***

Mike sat down at his computer and began an internet search on this carnival, "Julius is right; there isn't much information on this particular carnival. It's amazing how little there actually is."

Guy asked, "What about missing persons cases involving it?"

"It is difficult to tell, but it looks as if Julius may be right. I found two articles about people last seen at the carnival and never heard from again. I will call the police stations that handled those cases and confirm they are still missing. I also want to find out if they had any bodies turn up when the carnival was there. My gut tells me that there is something to this case."

"Yeah, mine too," Guy confirmed.

By the end of the day, Mike confirmed ten missing persons' cases where the last place they had been seen was indeed the carnival. One case went back as far as fifteen years, which made it hard to believe that a worker could be involved, but there was always a chance. It could be their guy started young and realized that since the disappearances were never discovered, he could continue. But if that was the case, there should be more missing persons' reports. Unless they were extremely careful and preyed on people who may not be missed. But then they would almost have to be mind readers. He didn't see how a fly by night carnival would know if someone would be missed or not. There were just so many possibilities with too few answers. However, he could not ignore the possibility that this was a potential case.

Mike handed Guy photographs of the missing persons, "I made these for you. We need to be on high alert in case one of these people are there."

Deciding to take Mike's vehicle, Mike drove so that Guy could study the photographs in more detail. Unlike Mike, he didn't have a photographic memory and wanted to memorize as many of the facial features of these people as possible. For the ones that had been missing for a while, it was next to impossible to envision what they'd look like. He would leave those to Mike for now. Mike had an eye for that sort of thing which made him a valuable addition to the team. If it looked like this was definitely something to pursue, then they could try the age progression software that he had invested in during a case a few years back. The software had turned out to be a good investment, and he had returned three missing teenagers to their parents.

As Mike drove to the carnival, he noticed how few businesses had rebuilt in this one particular area. It was depressing, actually. He wondered why the carnival elected to set up here. There wasn't as much traffic in this area to draw the crowds; however, when he saw the parking lot, he knew that word of mouth must have spread quickly. The parking lot was crazy, and there was absolutely no system in place for those coming or going. Cars lined the lot haphazardly. It was as if their owners just stopped where they wanted. When it came time to leave, it would be a living nightmare.

As he stepped out of the car, a gentle breeze greeted him. At least the weather was nice for a carnival. If they had waited for the summer months, it would have been too hot and humid for customers to enjoy the carnival. Besides, since they were only open at night, the mosquitoes would also be a problem. At least with the breeze and cooler weather, the mosquitoes wouldn't be out for blood tonight.

They joined the masses as they moved towards the entrance. To ensure they drew in the crowds, a man stood outside enticing people into entering. "Come see the freaks of the world's largest haunted traveling carnival! Beware of the fun house; you never know what horrors you will encounter. There are plenty of thrilling rides sure to make your heart stop."

There were two ticket booths set up at the front and both lines were long. Since neither of them were interested in the rides, they skipped the ticket booth and headed into the carnival. Mike did manage to secure a map of the grounds as they walked past the booths. This was the first time he had ever seen a carnival with its own road map, but he noticed the assortment of rides that it offered. It was far larger than he had anticipated, and he now knew why they needed the amount of room they had.   This carnival was packed wall to wall with people of all ages. All around him kids were screaming as they flew or hurtled through the air on the various amusement rides. The smell of popcorn and hot dogs along with body odor and perfume mingled in the air.

Guy smelled the air as well, "I smell nachos and funnel cake."

Mike shook his head, "I don't know how you can think of food right now. After looking at most of these workers, I'm not sure if I trust eating anything they cook."

Guy laughed, "You need to live in the moment mon ami. Besides, I'm sure that the health department has inspected everything."

Mike had loved the carnival as a child. His favorite ride had been The Sizzler; it spun you round and round, forward and backward. If he tried to get on the ride now, he had a feeling he would suffer from extreme motion sickness. Besides, when Guy drove back tonight, he was sure to have the ride of his lifetime. That man only knew one speed— fast. If it hadn't been because he had wanted to study the pictures before arriving, Mike would have been kissing the ground by the time they arrived. Watching trees zip past you at over one hundred miles an hour was not a pleasant experience.

Mike looked around, "So far it appears to be a typical carnival, minus the eerie décor."

Guy nodded his head in agreement, "Yeah. Did you see that carousel? It gives eerie a whole new meaning."

"Yeah, I guess kids only care about going round and round and aren't worried about the décor." The sleek black horses and red eyes were definitely unusual for a carnival. Even the music emitted from the ride was eerie.

As Guy listened to the music, he replied, "I swear the music coming from that carousel reminds me of a funeral march."

Mike watched a mom wave at her child as he went past on the carousel. Both of them looked so happy. What he wouldn't give for everyone in the world to be like that, no cares in the world.

Guy looked over at Mike, "So, how should we handle this?"

"Let's look around and see if anything jumps out at us. We should hold off asking too many questions right away."

Guy nodded his head in agreement, "That sounds like a plan to me." He pointed over to the big top, "Something tells me we may find some answers over there. They probably keep their secrets hidden in the back, away from the crowds."

As they passed The Sizzler ride, Mike noticed several women crowding the ride operator. There were even more women hanging over the metal railing surrounding the ride. Mike looked over at the ride operator and for the life of him couldn't figure out why the man drove these women wild. He watched the ride operator herd the people onto the ride. The women just stayed where they were instead of getting on the actual ride as if they were mesmerized by him. Mike had never seen anything like this before. As the operator started the ride, the huge round machine began to spin, forcing the people sitting against the wall to be pinned by the other passengers. The whole thing lifted off of the ground and made the riders believe they would fall which of course they wouldn't. The ride operator pushed a few buttons and the ride went even higher and faster. The people on the ride were screaming, but the women never took their eyes off the man; they could care less about the ride. Mike sure would like to know what the guy's secret was.

As they walked around the rides, they kept their eyes and ears open. So far, they hadn't found anything that would be useful regarding the missing persons' reports. As Mike watched the crowds, he realized just how perfect of an operation this would be for kidnapping, human trafficking, or murdering someone. They moved from town to town, grabbed a few people or murdered a few, and didn't even draw the attention of the local law officials before leaving. By the time it was discovered, the carnival was long gone and forgotten about.

As they walked around, Mike took a few pictures of the rides, of ride operators, and the crowd. The carnival was here for only a few days, so their time to figure out this mystery was limited. Unless they found out where they were going next and followed them. From what Julius said, though, that was almost impossible.

As they passed yet another ride, the operator called out, "Hurry, hurry, hurry. Step right up and give this ride a whirl." The man took the haunted theme to heart with the way he dressed entirely in black; he even had long sleeves. It may be Mardi Gras here, but with all these people around Mike wasn't sure if the long sleeves were necessary.

As they headed to the rear of the carnival where the trailers were, they heard someone holler from behind, "This area is restricted in case you didn't see the notices."

Mike turned around to see the man confronting them was a hulk of a man dressed in black. He took his part seriously; he looked very imposing.

Guy responded, "We are just looking around to see what else is here to see."

Mike had been taken by surprise when the man appeared behind them. He must be slipping because he didn't even hear him approach them. Mike took out one of the pictures he had of a missing boy, "Actually, we are looking for someone. A couple of parents believe that their son ran off to join your carnival after it came to their town. My partner and I are private investigators here in New Orleans. They asked if we could look around and find out if he is working for you. If he is, they just want to know, nothing more. They want to make sure that their son is safe and happy."

The man took the picture in his hand, but he shook his head, "I'm sorry, but I see hundreds of people a day. We haven't had any new hires in a while."

He handed Mike back the photo and escorted them to the main area of the carnival. Before they could respond, he disappeared. Guy replied, "Okay, that was a little strange don't you think?"

"Tell me about it. What about that guy's getup? He takes his part in this carnival a little too seriously."

"We need to get a better look around, but first we have to figure out where Mr. Creepy went."

"I never even heard him approach us. The guy moves quieter than a mouse."

Being careful and keeping a lookout for Mr. Creepy, they moved to the big top. Once there, they crept towards the back of it in search of a way in. They found a flap towards the back and slipped inside. If they were caught back here after being warned earlier, it would be hard to explain their presence once again.

When they entered through the back, they were consumed by complete darkness. It took a few moments for their eyes to adjust to their surroundings. Not wanting to be noticed, Mike took out his small pen light that gave them just enough illumination to see where they may be going. From where they were, he could see a narrow wall of canvas that led in one direction and to their left was a stack of boxes and crates piled high. The boxes and crates must be what they used to pack everything in. This left them one option, to follow the narrow walkway. If someone came across them in here, they had nowhere to hide.

The walkway led them to the main part of the tent where workers were busy with the sideshows and entertaining the audience. Being careful not to draw attention to themselves, they joined the crowd and watched the show. The main part of the big top consisted of several small stages set up to be used for each performer to show off their talent. If nothing else, he could say these carnies were efficient.

Mike looked around to make sure that Mr. Creepy wasn't nearby. Not seeing him, they moved on. Mike was surprised that there were this many acts; a rubber man who could twist himself into a small box that someone in turn picked up and carried around before he let himself out of the box again, and also a woman who stuck needles into her skin. There was a man who seemed to have a stomach made of steel as he ate glass and various other items. What side show wouldn't be complete without a bearded lady? There was even a wolf man. Guy whispered in Mike's ear, "I wonder if he howls at a full moon?"

They were watching one of the performers swallow fire when they felt a presence behind them. They turned to see Mr. Creepy behind them, "Are you gentlemen enjoying the show?"

Mike replied, "Very much so. I've never seen anyone as good as this performer."

"I don't recall seeing you two pass in front of me to get in here."

Guy responded, "Oh, didn't you? I'm not sure how you could have missed us. I believe my friend here even waved at you."

"Hmm, well it seems as if I would have noticed the two of you in this crowd. I hope you aren't here to cause trouble."

Mike shook his head, "Us? No, nothing like that. Like I said we came to look for the missing boy, but since you said you haven't seen him, we decided to take in the shows and sights while we were here instead of wasting a trip."

Mr. Creepy responded, "Now why don't I believe you?"

Guy shrugged his shoulders, "Mais, I don't know why you don't believe us. We aren't here to cause you any trouble. Besides, how can we come here and not enjoy the shows these fabulous performers are putting on?"

Mr. Creepy glared at them, "I think it is time for the two of you to find some other place to investigate. I don't want you to distract the workers or worry those that have come here to have a good time. I told you, I don't recognize the young man and we don't have any new hires. I feel sorry for this family, but you are looking in the wrong place."

As the creepy man walked away, the two friends looked at each other. Guy speculated, "I wonder why he is nervous about having us here. I think he wanted to escort us off the property and fast."

"Mais, this case is getting curiouser and curiouser."

As they continued to walk around the carnival, they paid particular attention to the carnival workers; making sure to hit every ride, game, and food booth. So far, they hadn't seen any of those missing or anything out of the ordinary, but they still couldn't shake the feeling that something was off here.

Guy let out a sigh, "This is turning out to be a bust."

"This case is turning into a puzzle and I don't like leaving a puzzle until it is finished. There is still one place that we haven't looked, and that is by the truck and trailers. Last time Mr. Creepy kept us from searching there."

"I say we take a look, but we need to keep a lookout for the man. I have a feeling he won't be as polite the next time he finds us snooping around."

Mike agreed, "It is in our best interest not to let him find us."

They stayed in the shadows as they moved quietly to the area where all the trucks and trailers were parked. Mike took his phone out and took pictures of the license plates. He would run those numbers to see if that helped in any way. As they wandered around, they listened carefully for any noise that sounded like someone being held against their will might make. They heard nothing but the sounds from the carnival.

Mike let out a sigh, "Well, this was another bust. Unless we feel like breaking and entering into the travel trailers, we got nothing."

From the corner of his eye, Mike caught a movement. He pulled Guy deeper into the shadows and put a finger on his lips before pointing to the area where he'd just seen a movement. The person was moving their way, and they hoped that he didn't notice them. As he walked by, Mike realized this wasn't a completely wasted trip after all. It appeared that one of their missing persons had indeed run off with the carnival. Before he could call out to the man, he disappeared into the night. Looking over at Guy, "Where did he go?"

Guy replied, "I have no idea, but I swear that guy looked like one of the photos we have of someone missing."

"He sure did. I would love to talk to him, especially after Mr. Creepy back there told us that he didn't have any new hires. He wouldn't hide the fact that he has new people working for him unless he had something to hide or maybe they do."

"I would like to come back here and look around during the daylight."

As they drove away from the carnival, Mike looked back at it one more time. From this distance, it took on an eerie quality. He wondered what secrets were trapped in those confines.

Mike pondered over how they could find out more about it, "If only we could look everywhere inside that carnival to see exactly what evil lurked there."

"Yeah, but something tells me they don't allow outsiders in there."

Mike ruefully agreed, "No, but I did see a lot of very attractive workers. Maybe we can befriend one of them and see if they will open up a little more."

Guy shook his head, "I don't know. The last time I tried that it nearly got my mole killed. I saved her just in time, and she is still in hiding."

"I know, but this may be our only way. We can't bring in the police or even the FBI without proof. Right now, they would laugh us out of the office. We have to dig into their past a little more and build up a story."

As they drove back into town, Guy's phone rang. It was his contact with the city permit's office. "Alicia, please tell me you found something for me to go on."

She sighed into the phone, "I'm sorry Guy, but I wasn't able to find too much information on the carnival. The carnival had filed for permits two weeks before they were due to set up. They had to pay a hefty fee for requesting permits so close to their arrival date. Since they agreed to pay the exorbitant fee, and they have come to New Orleans in the past, the Mayor and City Council didn't see a problem with approving the permits. You know the saying, 'Money talks and bullshit walks.' Well, that seems to be the case here. A Mr. Joshua Olivier signed the necessary permits, but that is where it gets a little strange. I did a search for Mr. Olivier and didn't find any information on him. It turns out that this particular traveling carnival registered with the State of Louisiana for a business license almost sixty years ago. I am guessing this Mr. Joshua Olivier is a Jr. or III and never updated any of the business records."

Guy interrupted, "So you are telling me that Mr. Olivier is the original owner of the company?"

She replied, "According to the business license department, yes, but as I said, that was sixty years ago. I am sure his son never bothered with a suffix after his name. It has been known to happen before."

After hanging up with Alicia, Guy told Mike everything that she had told him. Mike rubbed his chin as he listened to everything Guy had to say, "I say we find Mr. Joshua Olivier and see just how old he is."

Guy turned around and drove back to the carnival. After parking, they walked over to the ticket booth and asked, "Is Mr. Olivier here tonight?"

The ticket booth operator looked at them with clear hatred in his eyes, "And just who is asking?"

Guy pulled out his business card and passed it along to the ticket booth operator, "We just have a few questions about a missing person's report that was filed. He may be able to help us with some of the answers. The girl was last seen at this carnival."

With a sneer, the man informed them, "Mr. Olivier has stepped out for the night. He wanted to see the sights in New Orleans before we left. I believe he has family here, and that may be where he went, but it isn't my place to ask the boss questions."

Mike replied, "That is totally understandable. Please give him the business card and if he thinks of anything he can give us a call."

As they left, Guy asked Mike, "So, do you think Mr. Olivier has family here?"

Mike replied, "I think it may be something to look into."

Chapter 24

New Orleans, Louisiana
March 2013

Jeannie Easley sulked as she walked around the carnival. The noises from the carousel grated on her nerves. The flashing lights from the rides, the smell of cotton candy, corn dogs, and caramel apples from the food booths did nothing to improve her rotten mood.

She was supposed to meet her boyfriend here, but he texted her stating that he had to work late and couldn't make it. She decided to go and have a good time without him. However, instead of enjoying herself, she was miserable. She had no one to go on rides with and everywhere she looked she saw her friends walking hand in hand with their boyfriends. When they asked about Ryan, she had to tell them he was working late. What really got on her nerves, though, was that he could have easily told his boss he had other plans. His boss would have asked someone else to stay late, but no, Ryan would not do that. He never turned down the extra hours, even if that meant not being able to see her. All he cared about was saving up his money for some dumb car. She hoped that the car could keep him company at night because she was tired of playing second fiddle. There were plenty of guys out there, and she would find someone who treated her the way a girlfriend should be treated.

While kicking around rocks with her shoe, she walked right into someone. When she looked up, she found herself staring into an amazing pair of mesmerizing eyes. They were so black that they were hypnotic. Swallowing back her embarrassment, "Sorry. I wasn't paying attention to where I was going."

To help steady her, the man grabbed her shoulders, "That's okay. What is such a pretty girl like you doing all alone tonight?"

She replied without thinking, "My boyfriend bailed on me, and I'm not ready to go home just yet."

"Doesn't he know better than to leave a pretty girl like you stranded at the carnival? Another boy may move in and take his place."

She shrugged her shoulders, "His only concern is saving up for his stupid car."

She saw him shaking his head, "Well, if you were my girlfriend, I wouldn't let you out of my sight."

That brought a smile to her face, "I have a feeling your girlfriend wouldn't let you out of her sight either."

He placed a hand over his heart, "Unfortunately, working for the carnival doesn't leave much time for a girlfriend. We are always on the road."

She giggled, "Oh, that must be fun. Imagine all of the different places that you get to see and all the different people that you get to meet. Me, I have never been out of the city of New Orleans, much less the state. My parents don't like to travel; they are always saying that it costs too much money and that you never know who may have slept in the beds at hotels."

"I have a little time off; why don't I show you around the carnival? I can give you a new perspective."

Letting out another schoolgirl giggle, she replied, "Okay."

She followed him around, almost like a lost puppy dog. Now that she wasn't sulking anymore, she found the excitement around her contagious. She didn't need dumb old Ryan to have a good time after all.

They had to duck under wires strung precariously low in the rear of the rides. Whoever set this area up had apparently not planned on people walking behind here. They slipped between poles, dodging in and out of man-made alleys between the tents and vendor stands.

Even from where they were, she could hear the laughter around them. She hoped he was right, and they could get the best seat in the house to see the show under the big top. She peered into the crowd to see if there was anyone she knew; she wanted her friends to see her with this good looking man and tell her loser boyfriend. Maybe for once, he would get jealous and realize that if he didn't want her someone else would. Unfortunately for her, her friends ran right past her. They were only interested in the Tilt-A-Whirl they were headed toward. The dopes were probably hoping they would be the first in line for the next ride.

As they walked past a ride where the seats resembled cauldrons, something caught her attention. The way the ride operator was eyeing one of the kids gave her the creeps. Then again, it might be the way the children were sitting in giant cauldrons that made her uneasy. She looked around and for the first time she noticed how dark and eerie most of the rides were; however, everyone seemed to be enjoying themselves despite the creepy atmosphere.

As they passed the roller coaster, she let out a small shiver of fear. Waiting impatiently for their turn was a line of children, teens, and adults. The creepy roller coaster carts were made to look like black, shiny coffins. It went up a steep hill, before plunging into a dark tunnel that was lit only by black lights. She watched as the ride came to a stop, and the riders disembarked. She looked back because something wasn't right. She swore all the cars were full when the ride started, but now the second to last cart was empty. She looked around, but no one seemed to notice someone missing so maybe she was mistaken. Surely if someone had disappeared during the ride, someone would have noticed and said something.

She saw the good looking man further up ahead of her and hurried along to catch up. They entered the big top tent from the back, and before she knew it, someone pushed her into a crate and locked her inside. She felt around to find a way out, but found no means of escape so far. She pushed with all of her might on every side, but it was to no avail. She couldn't even find a door knob. She kicked and screamed at the top of her lungs, hoping that someone would hear her and come set her free. Her stomach filled with dread when she remembered that they had entered through the back of the tent where there was no one. No one saw her with the good looking man either.

Her mind kept going over all the things that could happen to her. She prayed that she wasn't about to be hurt. She had always had morbid thoughts about death, but now that it may be right at her door, she was afraid. She didn't want to die. She was too young; she hadn't had a chance to really live.

Suddenly, the crate opened. Shocked, she stared at the clowns and other carnival workers circling her. One of the ladies surveyed her up and down before walking up to her. Afraid to move, she remained frozen in place. The woman inhaled the air deeply around her and replied, "Mmmm, you smell good. I can't wait to see if you taste as good as you smell." When she smiled at her, she revealed her fangs. A chill pierced straight through to her very soul.

Suddenly, pain ripped through her body. Her neck felt as if it was on fire as the young woman's fangs pierced through the delicate area on Jeannie's neck.

Chapter 25

New Orleans, Louisiana
March 2013

In a rush to get home, Emily Stevenson decided to cut through the alley. Halfway down the alleyway, she heard a commotion and saw two men, cloaked in black, were having an altercation. Unsure of what to do, she ducked behind the dumpster and hoped that they quickly finished their business and left. One of them had an athletic build while the other was a heavyset, burly man.

She bit back a scream when the athletic man grabbed the other one with the speed of a cougar as he bent his neck back.

She was unsure what to do next. Who would believe her when she said she witnessed a murder? She prayed that the killer did not realize that she was hiding back here. It would mean certain death for her.

She shook her head as the realization of what she had witnessed took form in her head. This had to be a nightmare. Someone had to be pretending to be a vampire; after all, they only existed in the movies and books. Didn't they?

She crouched down lower as the killer moved her way. Her body shook violently with fear. Her heart pounded hard against her chest. For a moment, she thought it would beat right out of her. She clasped a hand over her mouth to silence her heavy breathing and prayed that he didn't see her hiding in the shadows.

As he walked by her, she leaned her head back against the brick wall and closed her eyes. Tears streamed down her cheeks.

***

When Detective Grace Hutcherson pulled up to the alley, the headlights of her car caught the crime scene tape and caused it to shine bright in the darkness. She hadn't been on the job long, and this would be her first murder case. She had thought New Orleans would be full of excitement and keep her busy with murder cases. However, since her arrival it seemed like the bad guys had taken a hiatus.

She'd left the small town of Jackson, Louisiana because of the lack of crime. She wanted to experience the rush of solving a murder and finding out exactly who did it. Although honestly, she had grown tired of small town life. She wanted to experience what other officers at the conferences had talked about. When she saw the job posting for a new detective here, she jumped on it. It took some convincing that she would fit in. The local sheriff and police commissioner didn't believe that she had enough experience, but they were trying to improve their public image and felt that hiring another female detective would help.

She didn't care why she had been hired. She knew that she could prove to everyone that she was perfect for the job. Even the sheriff for the town of Jackson hated to see her go, but supported her and gave her a glowing recommendation. She left on good terms, and he said that if she grew tired of big city life and the crime that went with it she'd always have a job waiting for her.

Her college professors and the instructors for the police academy had given her superb marks that helped immensely. They all praised her, stating that she was smart as a whip and perfect detective material. She wouldn't have made rank as fast as she did if she wasn't good at her job. She was thankful that the other detectives in the department had accepted her with no qualms. They had even taken to calling her by her nickname, Hutch, instead of newbie or fresh meat.

Hutch had a special gift that she could never explain. She had a way of reading people and scenes. The first accident scene she had ever worked no one could figure out how the car ran off the road, but she had sensed something when she had arrived. When she closed her eyes, she could feel herself being transported back in time. She could picture the accident happening. She was able to give her own account to the detective as they walked through the scene and found the skid marks that were almost invisible. It had been that way with the other accidents she worked as well. She could step back in time and watch it play out. Now if she only had the ability to warn people ahead of time, she could put this gift to good use.

As she arrived at this particular crime scene, her senses were on overload. There was something not quite right. She couldn't put a finger on it, but something in the air gave her the creeps. It was as if something very evil had been here and that some of it still lingered.

She'd felt this one time before, many years ago, when her aunt brought her to a carnival in a neighboring town. She had been so frightened that she didn't want to stay. After an hour of listening to her whine, her aunt caved in and brought her home. Her aunt kept asking what was wrong, but she just couldn't explain it to her. Her aunt harped on how most kids would be thrilled to go to a carnival and that she should have at least tried to have a little fun. When they got home, she confessed to her grandma that she just didn't feel comfortable there; her grandma told her always to trust her gut instincts. That was when her grandmother divulged that she had this special gift, and she should use it to keep herself out of danger. As Hutch grew up, her grandmother never did tell her too much about the gift; she only knew it was something special in the family and handed down only to the women.

Since this was her first time working with the responding officers and paramedics, she hoped that they didn't mess with the crime scene. Her partner, Detective Chance Benoit, had been with the force for a few years now and had seniority. She sometimes worried about his actual detective skills since he seemed only to be here for a paycheck.

Before the detectives went to check out the crime scene, they put on latex gloves and booties. They both ducked under the tape and headed towards the body. She noticed the techs were busy gathering what evidence they could. Detective Benoit must have sensed that she was nervous about the techs already working the scene and replied, "Don't worry Detective Hutcherson. They won't mess up our case. New Orleans has one of the best crime scene units in the state. They are used to dealing with murders and crime scenes on an almost daily basis. Even the district attorney's office and the judges say we have one of the most meticulous crime scene units statewide." That helped ease her nerves some. If she could vanquish the uneasy feeling about this whole scene, she would feel even better.

She couldn't shake the feeling that there was something unnaturally wrong about this place.

As they walked up to the body, one of the young paramedics looked at her and replied, "This case has some bad juju. The victim was dead, and you should hear what the witness has to say."

Hutch asked Dr. Ortego, the coroner, "What about the cause or time of death?"

"Well, according to the witness, your victim was murdered just a short while ago. Unfortunately, I won't be able to confirm that until I get him back to the autopsy table. Someone crushed his neck and drained his body of blood."

She asked, "What do you mean drained his body of blood? Here at the crime scene?"

"Yes, right here. The witness claims that the killer picked him up by his neck and drank his blood."

Detective Benoit shook his head, "Surely, she must be mistaken. He had to have used some kind of medical equipment to drain his blood."

She bent down and peered at the body. "There are two small puncture wounds on his neck and you can clearly tell the killer had a grip on his neck."

Dr. Ortego continued, "I need to check my records, but I don't believe that this is the first case New Orleans has had like this. It may have been some time back, but I know I worked a case very similar to this one before."

She nodded her head, "Okay Dr. Ortego. Just give one of us a call if you find anything." As she continued to inspect the body, she noticed a strange tattoo on the inside of the man's wrist, "Did you notice this?"

Benoit and Dr. Ortego looked down to see what she had found. Dr. Ortego informed her, "I believe I have seen this tattoo on a few other bodies, but I can't be sure. Most of them were probably drug overdoses, but I can find out for you. I have an assistant that catalogs tattoos. A lot of times, prisoners give themselves tattoos; if he has been in prison and the warden documented the tattoo, it should be in the system."

A shiver ran down her spine as a childhood memory surfaced about the carnival. She had no idea what brought it on, but she knew better than not to follow her gut instinct. A traveling carnival came into town last night, and now they had a mysterious death on their hands. This could be coincidence, but she wasn't one who believed in coincidences.

As they worked the scene and discussed the body, she tried not to think about this body as a person but as a case. She must remain professional and pragmatic. Just looking at the body, the only thing that came into her mind was a thug. No doubt, he finally pissed off the wrong person. If it weren't for the draining of the body, she would think this was a mob hit. She needed to look into that tattoo. Something inside of her told her that it was essential to this case. She also knew that the Mafia was prevalent here. The last detective had discovered that they had used voodoo to get to their enemies. She needed to look into the voodoo religion and see if there was any mention of exsanguinations in their rituals. The puncture wounds reminded her of the vampire movies that she was addicted to, which was ridiculous. Unless someone wanted to make it look like a vampire attack. She wondered if there was a vampire movie being filmed in the area and this was possibly a stunt gone wrong. Her mind was reeling with possibilities, and she needed to stay focused on the crime scene.

She walked to the other side of the alleyway and closed her eyes, allowing her mind to open up and see the scene as it was when the murder took place. She saw the victim enter the alley, but he was not alone. Another man, shrouded in darkness, was with him. As hard as she tried, she could not penetrate the darkness that surrounded him. Suddenly, something, or more importantly, someone invaded her thoughts. A voice filled her head, *"Leave this case be. This is of no concern to you cher!"*

She quickly opened her eyes and shook her head, trying to dislodge the voice. She wasn't sure exactly what just happened; she had never had anyone talk to her telepathically.

She had a feeling that the murderer may have made contact with her. She hadn't been prepared to deal with the invasion on her mind, but she would be next time. If only her grandma were still alive so that she could go talk to her. She would know how to advise her on handling this matter better.

***

Joshua was in his coffin when he felt the psychic's presence. He could tell that she was trying to read the most recent crime scene. He must find out more about her and see what she was up to. This was the first time since his existence he had someone reach him telepathically, and it had him intrigued.   Surely, a mere mortal couldn't have that much power. He tried to enter the person's mind again, but found that it was closed off. He had never had that happen, especially since his powers were so great. He would keep trying, just in case she opened up her mind once again. He intended to find out just who was attempting to solve this murder by supernatural means.

Chapter 26

Mike heard his phone ringing and thought it was a dream. Ever since he'd left the force, his phone seldom rang in the early morning hours, but he knew that a call this early wasn't good news.

He looked at the caller ID and saw that it was one of the EMTs he had met while working on the force. And wondered why he would call him at this hour.

He answered, "Bailey."

"Detective Bailey, this is Timothy Hebert. I don't know if you remember me or not, but we worked a few cases together in the past. Officer Rodriquez mentioned that you asked about any strange cases or missing persons' reports last night at the bar. Sir, I think I may have one that you will be interested in. The victim was drained of all his blood; his neck was crushed from whoever had a grip on him, and there were also two puncture wounds on his neck. The victim was a big man, and it would have taken a lot of force to hold him still long enough to drain his body of blood."

Mike knew well enough that the unexplained seemed to happen in New Orleans. When he was working on the force, they had tried to capture a voodoo priestess, Bianca, who had helped Dominic St. Germaine, the current mafia crime boss at that time. Somehow she kept vanishing into thin air. They couldn't find a prison around to hold her. He had suggested they pour a ring of salt around her, but the idea was scoffed at.

Even though they had yet another mysterious death, he didn't believe that voodoo was involved. The voodoo priestess was too careful to leave behind a body for anyone to find.

Timothy continued to talk, "The thing is, there is a witness who called the homicide in. The responding officer swears that she is drunk or high and refuses to listen to her. She is adamant that a vampire did this. She keeps telling him she knows that it is hard to believe, but she saw it with her own two eyes. She swears that she is clean, no drugs or alcohol."

Now this did have his attention. This mysterious death and the spotting of a "vampire" couldn't be a coincidence now that a strange carnival was in town. He learned a long time ago that there was no such thing as coincidences. Mike told Timothy, "I'm on my way, mon ami. Let me know if they take her to the station. I should make it there while they are still processing the scene. I don't live too far away."

"Yes, sir. I will keep you informed."

Mike would have to play this one low key. The investigating detectives wouldn't like that an ex-cop was also looking into one of their murders. If he was right and this did have something to do with the carnival in town, then this could be just what they needed to bring in the FBI. At least the FBI would have the manpower and resources required to work the case. He didn't believe that the carnival was actually run by vampires, but something about the place was off. He couldn't explain why the witness was fixated on the killer being a vampire, but when he was at the carnival, quite a few workers were dressed in gothic attire. Maybe that was what she saw, a worker dressed for the carnival.

That didn't explain how the guy's neck got crushed. He noticed quite a few workers there that could have the strength to do that though.

By the time Mike made it to the crime scene, multiple sets of flashing red and blue lights lit up the early morning sky. There were at least a dozen police cruisers, an ambulance, and the coroner's van parked near the alleyway. As he walked up to the officer in charge, he saw a white sheet draped over a body.

As he surveyed the crime scene, he saw uniformed officers and plain clothes detectives working. He saw Detective Benoit, but he couldn't get a good look at his new partner. On the other side of the alleyway, TV and news reporters were already gathering and being led away from the action. Why was there so much media attention and police presence for a simple homicide? Could it be that there was more to this than he thought or more than the paramedics even knew?

As he surveyed the scene, he saw a beat cop he knew and walked over, "Officer Melancon, do you have any idea who the victim is?"

He let out a laugh, "What's wrong Detective Bailey? You miss seeing dead bodies since leaving the force?"

"Oh, you know, now and then I miss the excitement of early morning calls and all."

"Yeah, right."

Mike chuckled, "I got a call that this death may be linked to a missing person's case I am working on."

"Yeah, well the victim was a bouncer at a club right down the road. At first they thought it was a hit, which is why everyone is here. Now they believe the guy ran into the wrong person in the alley."

"So, what made them think this was mob related."

"Just looking at the guy you would think Mafia, plus he has a strange tattoo on his wrist. He looks as if he could have walked directly off the set of one of those popular Mafia shows playing on TV."

Mike nodded his head as they watched the body being loaded up. He would give anything to look at it, but he knew that wasn't going to happen here. Maybe if he went straight to the morgue, Dr. Ortego would talk to him before the detectives arrived. From the looks of it, they would be here for a while. "What about the witness?"

Officer Melancon pointed over to one of the cruisers where she was sitting unguarded. "I don't think she saw too much and what she believes she saw doesn't make any sense. Turns out she knew the guy; he was a bouncer at the strip club where she works. He's paid to make sure the girls don't skip out without paying and to make sure no one causes trouble. Which means he has lots of enemies."

Mike walked over to talk to the witness while the detectives were busy. Since he didn't know the newest detective, he would call Benoit later on to follow-up. He had a good rapport with Benoit and should be able to get some more information from him.

Chapter 27

Hutch wasn't back at the office an hour when her office phone buzzed. "Detective Hutcherson, this is the front desk. I know that you don't work missing persons, but there is a family here insisting on talking to someone. Their daughter went to the carnival last night, and she hasn't returned home. It hasn't been twenty-four hours, but they are so distraught that I thought maybe you can explain to them that we have to wait forty-eight hours before we can do anything since she is over sixteen years old."

She asked, "Did you just say that she was last seen at the carnival?"

"Yes, ma'am. She was supposed to meet her boyfriend there, but he had to work and couldn't show up."

Hutch had a gut feeling that there may be something more to this carnival. Since its arrival to town, she not only had a mysterious death, but now possibly a missing girl.

She told the young officer, "Send them back."

She extended her hand to the parents as they approached her desk. "Hello, I am Detective Grace Hutcherson. I understand you want to report your daughter missing?"

The man grasped her hand and introduced himself and his wife, "I am Bill Easley and this is my wife, Connie. Our daughter, Jeannie, went to the carnival last night. She was supposed to meet her boyfriend there, but when we called him about midnight, he said he had called Jeannie and told her he had to work late. We tried calling her on her phone, but she isn't answering. We thought maybe she spent the night with one of her girlfriends, but they haven't seen her either. We finally got in touch with someone who saw her sulking around the carnival. They assumed that since her boyfriend wasn't with her that she was just upset. They did see her talking with another boy later that night. Jeannie has stayed out all night before, but she always comes home in the morning. This time she didn't."

Mrs. Easley chimed in, "She really isn't a wild child. She is just irresponsible at times. When she is out having a good time, she tends to forget to call and let us know where she is and what time she will be home. I have never worried about her in the past, but this time something is different. She always answers her phone whenever her father or I call. This time it goes straight to voicemail."

Hutch asked, "Do you mind giving me her number? I can have the cell phone company try to locate her by the GPS chip."

Mr. Easley replied, "Sure." He wrote it down on a piece of paper for her and handed it to her.

She asked, "Do you have a picture of your daughter?"

Mr. Easley handed her a few photos, "These are all recent."

Hutch informed them, "Normally, we have to wait forty-eight hours before we can investigate a missing person's case; however, certain circumstances can warrant us to start an investigation sooner." She left out the fact that, unfortunately, their case was not one of those, but she would take it upon herself to go check out the carnival tonight. She took out one of her business cards from her desk and handed it to Mr. Easley. "This is my business card. If you hear from your daughter, or her friends, please let me know immediately. I will give you a call if I find out something. The best thing you can do is go home in case your daughter comes back or tries to call you. Please let me know immediately if that happens."

***

Hutch sat down at her computer to see what information she could find out about this traveling carnival. She also wanted to see if there were any missing person's reports filed in the cities they had visited. If he had kidnapped people along the way, how was he moving them? What were the various ages and sexes? Human trafficking usually involved women and children, not men. Maybe the man killed was part of a group that helped transport the kidnapped victims. She needed to ask Benoit if he'd found out anything about the tattoo.

She knew that most human trafficking victims were sent out of the country. The rich foreign nationals didn't care about the cost or how slaves were obtained; all they cared about was having a plaything. Human trafficking had been around for years and so far the authorities had been unable to stop it.

She looked down at her watch and noticed that it was already after six o'clock in the evening. The carnival should be getting ready to open in the next hour or so. She found herself being strangely pulled to the carnival. Something in her gut told her that she should go check things out on her own, to get a feel for the place.

After listening to the witness swear that a vampire killed their murder victim and the arrival of the carnival coinciding with the discovery of the body, it would be negligent on her part not to follow up on this lead.

As soon as she walked through the entrance, she was met with eerie music playing so loud that it vibrated her bones. She wondered how anyone could enjoy themselves with the music that loud.

As she walked by the carousel, she was unexpectedly overwhelmed with childhood memories.

She was at the carnival with her aunt. She could hear the music and the laughter of the other children as they ran around. There was the aroma of popcorn, cotton candy, hot dogs, and funnel cakes. Her aunt was nagging her about whining and how she should be thankful to be at the carnival. No matter how hard her aunt pushed, she couldn't shake the feeling of dread that had overwhelmed her.

Everything that was happening now seemed to be the same as in the past. She had a difficult time deciphering between the two.

As her aunt was dragging her to the carousel, a scary man walked near them. She grabbed hold of her aunt's hand even harder and refused to let go. Something about him made her uneasy. His eyes were as black as night, except when he looked at her they glowed red.

When she looked back, the man had disappeared, and she was on the carousel. As it started to turn, it began slowly at first and then became faster. These horses weren't the same cheerful ones like other carousels she had been on. No, these horses were scary and black. They seemed to be

Hutch shook her head, trying to bring herself out of her
reverie. Something about that memory wasn't right. That's
not what happened, but for the life of her, she couldn't
remember why she was scared of the carnival back then
and why she had insisted on leaving the carnival at once.

As she walked by the fun house, the barrier that she had
been keeping up was forced open. For a moment, she
attempted to talk to whoever was trying to read her mind.
She told him, "I know you are here." Suddenly, as if
someone was slamming a door shut, the intruder left her
thoughts alone.

***

Joshua knew that she was here, but he wasn't prepared for
her to announce that she knew he was here. Could it be
that she knew what was going on? She was very good at
keeping her mind blocked, but she wouldn't be able to keep
him out of her thoughts forever. He would wait for her to
fall asleep. He doubted she could keep her guard up all
night long.

***

Ashley's hands shook as she closed the cash drawer and gave the handsome man his change. She saw him here on opening night and knew that his presence made the master of ceremonies nervous. That was a first for her; she had never seen him nervous before.

Mike leaned in to play the game, sensing that something had the young woman uneasy. This may be just the person he needed to talk to, "What is your name?"

She hesitated only briefly before responding, "Ashley."

"Well, Ashley, have you worked here long?"

She shook her head. She wanted to warn him to stop asking questions and to get out of here. He needed to leave and never look back. She may think the words, but she would never let them pass her lips. She really should be careful with her thoughts. She didn't want Joshua to hear what she was thinking. Just because he wasn't right here with her didn't mean he couldn't see or hear her. She saw one of the dogs walking around earlier, so she knew he had them on the prowl tonight. This man must have really made him uneasy to have the shape shifters working in shifts. They usually guarded the area by day and slept at night, but not lately. He had them working around the clock, roaming the carnival and blending in with the locals. "I have only worked here for a few months."

He took out a flyer from his back pocket and showed it to her, "I am looking for this young girl. Have you seen her?"

She looked at the picture and fully understood why the master was so nervous. This man was looking for a missing young girl, one whose very soul was trapped here. If he was asking about her, could he already know that several disappearances may be linked to them? If so, it could prove to be detrimental to him, or to all of them, and yet, she wanted to help the one person who could end her very life.

A chill washed over her as if someone was watching her. She looked over her shoulder to see if anyone was lurking about in the shadows. In the distance, she could see the red glowing eyes of one of the Rougarou studying her every move. Could it be that the master knew? No. If he had known what she was thinking, she wouldn't be here. He would have ended her very existence the moment he learned about her pending betrayal and not once would he have asked if he had misread her thoughts.

Not trusting the ears around her, she looked deeply into his eyes and for only a moment let the wall around her thoughts slip. She hoped that he could read her thoughts, *"Unsafe here. Meet me in my trailer come daybreak."*

***

When the young girl looked directly into Mike's eyes, he felt himself being drawn in. A rush of thoughts ran through his mind, but only one was very clear. For just a moment, he was unsure of what he thought he heard, but when he looked at the girl and she lifted her chin, he knew she'd just sent him a message. This case was getting strange, but he refused to give up. He knew that the answers were here and come daybreak, he would visit this young woman's trailer to see what she had to tell him.

An uneasiness came over him, and he felt like he was being watched. Looking around, all he saw was a gorgeous black dog that reminded him of a wolf or a wolf hybrid. Why would anyone have a wolf running lose where children were at play? He could understand while the carnival was closed they may need security, but a wolf was a little excessive.

***

The alpha Rougarou watched as the man tried to get answers from the young charge. He would watch this one closely. He howled into the night, calling one of his pack to come and watch her while he followed the man. He wanted neither out of their sight. He would have to report his findings back to his master later.

He slipped into the shadows and shape shifted into human form to blend into the crowd. This made it easier to follow the man with too many questions. Even he could feel a change in the air. A shift in power was coming, one that they must prevent at all costs.

There were times when the alpha wanted to be released from his bonds, but that would never happen. Once the master had you under his control, there was no relinquishing it. He never set any of his charges free, except through death. That was not something he wanted. No, instead this small clan of Rougarou had been cursed into servitude to this coven for almost a century now.

He used to dream of escape knowing it was impossible. The master would just hunt him down and kill him, sending a clear message to the rest of his pack. He wondered what his life would have been like if he had not been forced to live this nightmare. Regardless of what went on in the lives of the pack, they were bound to serve the master.

Chapter 28

Hutch screamed out, "NO!" She wasn't sure how long she had been asleep when she bolted upright in bed. Her nightgown was soaked with perspiration, and her heart felt as if it would beat out of her chest.

It took a moment for her to realize she was safe and sound in her own bed. She let out a sigh, reminded herself that it was only a dream, as her surroundings once again became familiar.

She still couldn't shake the feeling that it was more than a dream. She dreamed that she was back at the carnival, only this time she was inside the fun house. She was trapped inside a maze of mirrors, but when she reached out to touch them, they were more like a thin plastic. Instead of her face looking back at her, there were the faces of men, women, and children trapped behind the mirrors. They were calling out to her, begging to be set free. The first time this happened had been when she visited the carnival with her aunt. She had never breathed a word about what happened that day to anyone, not even her grandma knew. While at the carnival, she decided to go into the fun house and check out the mirrors the other kids had been laughing about. Her curiosity had gotten the best of her, and she wanted to be like everyone else and have fun while there. She assumed something must be wrong with her, that there was nothing evil in the carnival. If there was something evil, none of the parents would allow their children to run free. As soon as she entered the fun house, a strange feeling came over her. When she walked into the hall of mirrors, she became frightened to death. The other kids were laughing at their funny reflections, but instead of her reflection she saw strange faces crying and pleading for help. No one else could hear their pleas. When a creature in the mirror reached out to touch her, she jumped and ran without ever looking back. The voices in her head did not stop asking for help until they were far from the carnival.

She hadn't thought about that fearful night since then. It must have been the recent trip to the carnival that brought back the memories. Something told her she should visit the fun house again; that may put her fears to rest.

As she fell back asleep, her phone rang. She let out a low groan when she saw it was the dispatcher. Looking at the time, it was well past seven in the morning. She must have been in a deeper sleep that she thought and slept through her alarm.

***

Joshua, however, had a wicked smile on his face. The foolish girl didn't realize that when she slept her guard was down. He invaded her dreams and saw her biggest fear. She had the power to see the souls trapped in the mirrors. It may be time for her to join them. It wouldn't do for her to start putting things together and realize that there were souls trapped in there. He would lose his powers if they were set free.

He went to sleep knowing tonight he would have a big meal waiting for him. He wondered what kind of powers he would gain when he stole the soul of Grace Hutcherson.

Chapter 29

New Orleans, Louisiana
March 2013

Mike reentered the carnival as daybreak came, wondering why he was here. As he walked by the now darkened ferris wheel, he noticed the mess made from last night's crowd. He would hate to work on the crew that had to clean this place up. They would have an all day job.

As he made his way to the now silent Tilt-A-Whirl, he noticed for the first time just how garish the carnival looked in the daylight. There were signs for CORNDOGS! COTTON CANDY! CANDY APPLES! FUNNEL CAKES! BLOOMING ONIONS! He wondered how many kids left here with belly aches last night.

As he made his way to the trailers where the workers slept, a scream came from the fun house.   He walked in and found himself in a tunnel draped with fake cobwebs. Up above, black lights helped create the perfect eerie mood to go with the green glowing skulls and crossbones on the walls. He listened carefully to see if this was where the scream had come from. Not hearing any noise, he left and headed for the trailers.

***

When Mike made it home, he was greeted by one of the most gruesome sights he had ever seen in his career, which spoke volumes. Now, he wished he had convinced the young girl into coming with him and going into hiding.

He pulled out his phone and called the 911 dispatcher to let her know that a murder had taken place. They needed to send a detective, the crime scene unit, and coroner to his house. He knew better than to touch anything and waited for the police to arrive.

When he saw the new detective stepping out of the car, his breath caught. If he had known she would be coming to work in the department, he might have stayed on. He grinned when he saw that she had been partnered with Detective Chance Benoit.

***

Hutch looked around the crime scene before moving in to examine the body, paying special attention to the bystanders. Sometimes the killer liked to watch firsthand when the police investigated the crime scene. She would make sure the crime scene photographer took pictures of everyone on the streets.

***

As the new detective studied the crowd, Mike took this opportunity to study her. What he wouldn't give to run up to her and remove that ponytail from her hair to see just how long it was. From what he could tell, it was a vibrant auburn. Even pulled up, her highlights glimmered in the morning sun. When she turned and looked his way, he noticed that she had the most gorgeous green eyes he had ever seen. Her face appeared flawless and had full, pouty lips that begged to be kissed.

She wore a black leather jacket over a white turtleneck with skin tight black jeans that were tucked into a pair of black boots. He could see her on the back of a motorcycle.

Hutch watched intently as Chance walked up to the man standing near the crime scene and shook his hand like they were old buddies.

Chance asked Mike, "What are you doing here? I thought you gave up the crime scene business?"

Mike shook his hand in return and laughed, "This house happens to be mine."

"Seriously! Well, who did you rub wrong this time? Are we dealing with another Mafia matter?"

Mike shook his head, "No, I don't think this has anything to do with the Mafia. I do believe that it may have something to do with a case I am currently working on. I have been hired to look for a missing girl. She was last seen at a traveling carnival here in town."

Hutch caught the end of the conversation and asked, "So just how does a body being drained of blood and staked on your front lawn connect with a missing person's case? This seems a little brutal for a simple missing person's case."

Mike nodded his head in agreement, "I think this case is a lot more sadistic than just a simple missing person's case. The young woman you see staked on my front yard was an informant I talked to only a few hours ago. She refused my offer to protect her; she said that no one could keep her safe if they found out she talked to me. Something tells me her boss found out."

Hutch asked, "So, you think that her boss had her murdered just for talking to you about a missing person's case?"

"Like I said, I don't believe that this is just a simple missing person's case. I have done my research, and there are several more missing persons' cases along with a few unsolved murders that correlate with the time frame when the traveling carnival is in certain towns. The young lady came forward to tell me that she suspected someone with the carnival has been murdering victims along the way and disposing of their bodies at the carnival."

Hutch asked, "Did she happen to have any proof to substantiate her thoughts?"

"Unfortunately, she did not. She did suggest that I make an anonymous call to the health department and have someone check out the food vendors that worked for the carnival."

Benoit stepped in, "Are you suggesting that she felt the bodies were being used as meat in the carnival?"

Mike nodded his head, "That was her belief, yes."

As they were talking, Dr. Ortego walked over to them, "Mike it's good to see you again. I wish it were under different circumstances."

Mike nodded to the coroner, "Same here Dr. Ortego."

Hutch asked, "What can you tell us Dr. Ortego?"

"I won't know the time of death until I perform the autopsy. But I can tell you her body was completely drained of its blood. This young woman was tortured before being killed. Some of the wounds were starting to heal, but it looks as if a dog recently attacked her. There were deep gouges on her body that looked like claw marks."

As Mike listened to the doctor, he cringed. Guilt washed over him and settled deep in the pit of his stomach. He should have picked her up kicking and screaming from that trailer and done everything in his power to keep her safe.

As they were talking, one of the crime scene techs walked over to the detectives, "Detective Hutcherson, I thought you would like to know that we did get a match on the fingerprints for the victim. But ma'am, something isn't quite right."

She asked, "What do you mean something isn't quite right? It wasn't a positive match?"

"Well, when we ran the fingerprint scan through, it came back fairly quickly. She was reported missing several years back. Her name is Ashley Welsh, but that isn't what has us stumped. You see, she was reported missing almost ten years ago, and she hasn't aged one bit. Except for the fact that she is dead, she looks exactly like her picture did back then."

Hutch looked at the information on the tablet he handed her, "Maybe the missing person's database messed up on her case. It could be that they inadvertently added her age progression photo instead of her original."

The young technician shook his head, "I don't think so. The rest of the information matches, but I will call them to be sure."

Benoit instructed the technician, "Why don't you email me that information on the missing person's case and I will call the detective who worked the case. He may be able to enlighten us."

Benoit then looked at Mike, "Was this one of the missing persons you were looking for?"

He shook his head, "No, she wasn't. As a matter of fact, I didn't see her name come up on any of my lists regarding missing persons and the carnival."

Hutch handed him the tablet with the information, "No, it doesn't mention anything about a carnival in the report. It said she just never came home."

***

As Mike read over the report, he didn't see any of the same links that he had found in the other missing persons' cases. He wondered how Ashley managed to get mixed up with this crowd. Could it be that she had been lured into the carnival by someone after she had been turned? When he talked to her, he could hear a lot of regret and guilt in her voice.

As Mike listened to the two detectives and coroner speak about the mysterious cases, he kept his mouth shut. He had no desire to tell them that they died from a vampire bite or that the reason Ashley Welsh hadn't aged since she went missing was because she was a vampire too. No, if he told them that, there was a good chance that they would think he had gone over the deep end and would have him committed. No, it was best to keep this information confidential for right now. He would wait to see if they came to the same conclusions.

As Dr. Ortego's assistants carefully removed the silver chains draped across Ashley's body so that she could be loaded onto the gurney, the body burst into dust. An overwhelming sense of remorse washed over him. He'd caused her death. He may not have been able to prevent it, but he would do everything in his power to make sure her murderers were found and stopped. However, for him to accomplish that, he needed to know how to kill a vampire. Obviously silver had something to do with harming a vampire. Was this what prevented her succumbing to an immediate death?

Hutch asked, "Did you find anything that we could use to get a search warrant for probable cause or evidence?"

Mike replied, "No."

Benoit suggested, "Maybe if we ask nicely they will let us take a look around."

Mike shook his head, "I wouldn't count on it. The guy that runs the carnival looks to be mighty tough. Something tells me that he won't cooperate with us."

Hutch stated, "I'll do a background search on this carnival and see if there is any more information that I can pull up."

Mike informed her, "I already tried to do a background search and strangely, I wasn't able to pull up too much information."

Hutch smiled at him and winked, "I may have a few contacts that you don't know about. When I was living in Jackson, I helped an IRS agent with a ticket, and he owes me a few favors."

Mike was impressed, "Oh yeah? That may prove to be very useful. I wasn't able to get anywhere with the tax records."

Chapter 30

New Orleans, Louisiana
March 2013

Mike pulled up the morning's online paper to see if the recent murder had made the front page news. As the page loaded, he could see the headline and knew it had, which meant the New Orleans Police Department had their hands full. Even though they warned them to leave the investigating to them, Mike and Guy took this murder personally. They refused to stop investigating the carnival, the missing persons' reports, and the rash of gruesome murders that had suddenly plagued this city.

They were getting close to solving the case, and it was spooking someone.

Once the article was downloaded, he read it.

Gruesome Murderer Strikes the City

A most revolting and fiendish murderer struck this fair city early this morning. A young woman was found staked in front of the residence of a former New Orleans police detective's home today. Detective Mike Bailey made a name for himself with the department when he put away one of New Orleans' prominent residents, Dominic St. Germaine, revealing that not only was St. Germaine the head of the Mafia here in New Orleans but had committed several murders. St. Germaine was also involved in human trafficking. With the help of Guy Mayon, they not only solved the case, but rattled the city when it was revealed that the Mafia had several politicians along with officers in the police department on their payroll.

Not wanting to read anymore, Mike closed out the site. As much as he hated to believe in the supernatural there was no denying the facts. He had a feeling they were dealing with more than the usual killer.

*****

At the same time that Mike pulled up the online article, so did Joshua. He couldn't wait to see the headline about the happenings of this morning's finding. He had to leave most of the details to his alpha male, and he hoped that he carried out his orders as instructed.

A wicked smile formed on his face. His plan was coming to fruition. He had heard people whispering on the streets about the previous murder and was thrilled to find that was included in this article as well. He had everyone in New

Orleans talking about the possibility of vampires. Now, to make sure that this duo of private investigators got the message and left well enough alone.

***

Guy was opening the office when the phone rang. He rushed to answer it and saw it was Julius Williams. "Mr. Mayon, I know you said to give you some time to look into the matter, but I was hoping maybe you had found out something by now."

"Mr. Williams, I realize that you are anxious to find your sister and I promise you we are looking into the matter, but it may take some time. Both my partner and I believe that there is something fishy going on at the carnival. We did not see Amber there, but we did locate one young man who had been reported missing from another state."

Julius let out a gasp, "Are you able to bring in the police?"

"Not at this time. The young man disappeared before we could ask him any questions. From the way he was acting, though, he more than likely ran away with the carnival when it came to his town. If he had been kidnapped, he wouldn't have run off like he did when we spotted him."

Julius continued to ask questions, "So what makes you think that something fishy is going on there?"

Guy explained, "When I asked the owner if he had hired anyone recently, he lied and said no. Not only did we see the young man recently reported missing, but the guy didn't like us asking questions around there. I have a feeling we made him more than a little nervous. Don't worry, though, we have no plans on giving up anytime soon. Mike and I believe that as long as the good people here in New Orleans keep spending their money at the carnival they will continue to stay open. I have done my research, and it appears that every year they return for Mardi Gras."

Julius asked, "Have any disappearances been linked here to the carnival?"

"That is hard to answer since Mardi Gras is wild, and the options are endless as to what could have happened to someone during this particular time frame. To answer your questions though, there have been missing persons' reports filed at Mardi Gras, but like I said, it will be hard to link any of those to this carnival. I will inform you as soon as I have something concrete to go on."

Julius was silent for a moment before saying, "Thank you for your help. I really do appreciate it. I am sorry if it seems like I am pestering you, but I just can't go home without knowing."

Guy knew that Julius was upset and worried, but right now, he just didn't have any definitive answers. Something told him that it wouldn't be long before he did though.

No sooner than Guy hung up with Julius, his cell phone rang. "Mike, what's up?"

"We need to talk. I know for certain now that there is something evil going on at the carnival, but I may have messed up big time. My informant refused protection and she is now deader than she was when we talked this morning."

"What do you mean she is dead?"

"Well, she worked for the carnival and refused my help in trying to hide her. She informed me that we couldn't keep her safe from her master. Her best bet would be to stay put and hope that he didn't know she talked to me. I'm guessing somehow he found out since I found her staked on my front yard as a warning. When they tried to move the body, it exploded into dust. We are dealing with the paranormal here. I don't know how to tell you this other than coming right out and saying it, but we are dealing with vampires. Not humans acting like vampires, but actual vampires."

Guy let out a loud chuckle, "Mon ami, you have been listening to your EMT buddy just a little too much lately. The voodoo priestess I can buy and the zombies have been explained by the drug she was using from Haiti, but vampires? That is just too hard to believe. Now, I am concerned about the witness you spoke with being staked for all to see on your front door step. That isn't good Mike!"

Mike let out a disgruntled sigh.   "Guy, I am telling you that this case is way bigger than we initially thought. The carnival is a cover for a cult of murderous vampires that steal souls. What makes it worse is the way they dispose of the bodies. They process them into the meat for the food they serve at the carnival."

Guy made a gagging noise when he heard Mike talk about the food. "So, let me get this straight. The carnival is run by vampires who not only kill their victims, but serve them up as dinner for the customers."

Mike confirmed this, "Yes. She went into detail about their criminal behavior, something that she was not proud of, by the way. She said that she was putting herself in grave danger just by talking to me, that her master has psychic abilities. She swore that no one could protect her. Her only chance was to pretend that nothing was out of the ordinary until we moved in and came to save the day. She instructed me that if I just thought of her name then her master would know that we had talked."

Guy ran his hands through his head, "I don't know mon ami. This is just too hard to believe."

Mike explained, "The best way to prove what I am saying is for us to go back to the carnival during daylight hours, but we may want to invest in some holy water and a crucifix. Let me know if you have anyone, anyone at all, stop by and ask to speak to me or if you see someone from the carnival. You must keep your thoughts guarded too. I have learned quite a bit these last few hours."

Guy still couldn't believe his ears, "Come on man. You're pulling my leg."

Mike informed his friend, "Forget about what you think you know about vampires. Most of the stuff in the movies is bullshit from what I have learned. Vampires can walk in the daylight, but if they do, they must wear sunscreen and dress heavily to protect their skin. It also seems that our group of vampires has guard dogs. Remember the wolves that we saw that night at the carnival?"

"Yeah, I remember. What about them?"

"They can change into human form or, if I understood her correctly, whatever form they need to get their job done. They usually sleep during the night and guard the vampires during the day, but that is not always the case. As a matter of fact, I think the guard dogs are the ones who did the dirty work with regards to disposing of the body on my front yard. Guy, you have to be extremely careful. They can take any form, so you need to make sure that the person who comes to visit you really is that person. If you see me, you need to make sure that it is me, okay? If they can kill one of their own, then just think of what they will do to someone who is threatening their very livelihood."

Guy wasn't sure what to believe, but it wasn't like his friend to make up extravagant stories. To be on the safe side, he would take heed to his warnings. "Okay, Mike, when do you want to go back to the carnival?"

"I want to go back as soon as we can. I have already let the detectives know that the young girl found murdered on my front yard worked for the carnival and that we were investigating several disappearances that may be linked to them. This is going to be a tricky situation though. Right now, the police don't know what to think about any of this, especially with the body disintegrating in front of their very eyes. I didn't bring up the word vampires to them because I knew they would laugh and lock me up in the loony bin. They did listen when I told them that she had just talked to me a few hours ago. They were quick to concede that someone may have been upset that she spoke to me. Something tells me that they won't find any evidence at the carnival regarding her murder or any murder for that matter. I did suggest that they should send someone from the health department over to the carnival to check the meat they were using. We will just have to wait and see if that happens."

***

As soon as Mike hung up, his cell phone rang again. It was the New Orleans Police Department, "Bailey."

"Mike this is Detective Hutcherson. I plan on heading over to the carnival today to see what I can find during the daylight hours. We will be making another trip tonight, but sometimes it pays to have a lay of the land before getting down to the nitty-gritty."

"I can go with you since I have been there before."

"Actually, I was there last night, but now that I know what I am looking for, it could have different results."

"I am surprised you went to the carnival last night. I didn't take you for a carnie groupie."

She laughed, "I went to check it out since we had a murder that I believe could be linked to someone at the carnival."

"So you do suspect that a worker is guilty of the first murder? I was wondering about that."

She replied, "Right now, it is just a hunch. I find it too coincidental that a mysterious murder occurs at the same time a mysterious carnival arrives in town."

"Hmm, maybe you are a cracker jack detective. I suspect the same thing. There were plenty of workers dressed like vampires when I was there, but that isn't enough to get a search warrant."

She agreed, "No, it isn't and whoever killed the first victim, and Ashley, didn't leave us too much evidence to go on. It will be difficult to prove that someone at the carnival may be involved. They cover their tracks very well."

"Okay. I will meet you at the carnival say, in an hour?"

She replied, "That works for me."

***

Before leaving, Hutch went in to brief the sheriff where the case stood and what she had planned. He informed her, "Go check it out, but you must be very careful. I think we may be able to push a sting operation on the carnival tonight if I can get everything arranged from here. The mayor is still uncomfortable with everything that has happened in the past few months. As soon as I mention the words human trafficking, I don't see a problem with him strong arming a judge into signing a simple warrant for us to look around. If you go there today and find something that gives us probable cause, it will just solidify the warrant."

On her way to the carnival, Hutch called Mike and told him, "We may be able to get a sting operation to go down tonight. The sheriff wants to see what all I find there today to help push the warrant through. He doesn't think it will be a problem getting it pushed through the red tape regardless of what I find though. I guess since your last case all he has to do is mention human trafficking and he will get everything we need."

***

Mike couldn't believe that he had the police involved this early in the investigation. He figured it would be like pulling teeth to get something done. Maybe, solving the Mafia case did help matters some regarding getting warrants pushed through. Either way, he would take the help. Now, he had to figure out how in the world they could protect themselves from vampires.

***

Tyler witnessed what happened with Ashley, and he knew that they must leave, and they must leave now! He had had a sense of impending doom, and it grew stronger every day. He waited in the trailer for Josie. Earlier today, he'd found an abandoned house that had a cellar that they could hide out in.

As soon as she opened the door, he pushed her inside, "We have to go now. There is no time to explain."

Josie looked up at him with love visible in her eyes, "I would follow you to the ends of the earth. I trust you completely."

As he pulled her out of the trailer, he told her, "I have already moved what I could to our hiding spot. I wasn't able to take much without bringing suspicion to my activities. Daylight will soon be here, we must go."

Chapter 31

New Orleans, Louisiana
March 2013

Joshua had had a long night and even longer morning. They would leave New Orleans in a few days. While he would like to stay longer, there had been too many people asking questions lately.

All he wanted to do was crawl into his chamber and fall fast asleep. The nosey private investigator was spotted asking questions again tonight. Even after the warnings, he had yet to let the matter drop. To make matters worse, he confirmed that Ashley had indeed informed the investigator of everything that went on here. She forgot to listen to her own warnings about his shape shifters. The Rougarou that found out about her deceit had been rewarded with a move up In rank and given the privilege of ending the betrayer's life.

Her death was a warning to that nosey investigator, and any of his children that thought of deceiving him. Now, they would think twice about ever crossing him.

As he opened the door to his trailer, he sensed another presence there. It was definitely human, but also something more.

Unsure of what he would find, he bared his fangs and prepared to take a life. Sitting at the small table in the middle of the room was a woman who took his breath away. She had long black hair and the greenest eyes he had ever seen.

He asked, "What are you doing in here?"

Instead of answering, she just laughed at him. It was a carefree sound that put him at ease. She stood up, unafraid of his appearance. "I've been waiting for you to return. Did you have a good supper tonight?"

Could it be this woman had figured out exactly what he was? Without waiting for him to respond the lady said, "My name is Queen Bianca. You and I are about to become best friends. For you see, I can keep you safe from those that are searching for you. As far as your children, I am afraid there isn't much I can do for them. We may be able to help a few, but some here I don't trust."

"You think someone in my flock is betraying me?"

"Mais oui. I have read your cards and knew one of your followers means to cause you harm. Before that can happen, let me help you."

"And why would a mere mortal want to help me? More importantly, what makes you think I need the help of a human?"

She let out a seductive laugh, "Oh cher, I am so much more than a mere mortal. With my help, you can achieve all your dreams. We can create an army of zombies and vampires that will help us take over the world."

"And pray tell, how do you plan on creating an army of zombies?"

Bianca asked, "When you take a soul, you power your carnival, mais oui?"

"Just so we are clear in our understanding, my betrayer has already been dealt with. Did she tell you about how I power my carnival or do I have another traitor in my midst? I want to know who is divulging my secrets. I will deal with their disloyalty quickly."

She stood up and placed a hand on his shoulders, "Relax. I know many things. Somehow, I never knew of your existence until the recent newspaper articles, but now that I do, I plan on making sure that you see things my way. I am sorry that I did not get here in time to warn you of the betrayal though."

"And what happens if I refuse to join forces with you?"

She replied, "I am certain that there are those in New Orleans that would love to put the monster murdering people here behind bars. You see those same men have been trying to put me behind bars too. It's just that I am too quick for them. There is no place that they can put me that I will stay in. My powers have grown so that it is quite easy for me to transport to many places with ease."

He asked, "Just exactly what are you lady?"

"I am a voodoo priestess, one to be feared by mere mortals and the likes of you as well."

Over the centuries, he had heard of voodoo, but he had never met anyone that practiced the mysterious religion. "And you believe voodoo will help me?"

Talking with her hands, she replied, "Mais oui cher, most definitely. I can teach you how to do things you would never have dreamed of, like how to turn your lost souls into zombies. You can control them to do your bidding whenever you wish, much better than your children. I have to use my powers to turn them into zombies, but you can do it with a single bite. I envy that in you.”

“So, you practice more than just white magic?”

Her laugh turned more sinister this time. He noticed a shift in her energy, “You have no idea what I can do. I may have been forced into hiding in the swamplands, but that doesn’t mean I haven’t been practicing my voodoo. I have continued to strengthen my powers and my flock.”

He studied this mysterious woman who claimed to be a Voodoo priestess. Was someone else betraying him? Who among his children would do this? Who was strong enough to hide their true intentions? He had a psychic bond with all, except for the one he rescued and he had already taken care of her. Wait. Could it be her? She had been such a lost child when their master turned her; she had been unsure of this life. He had taught her so much over the years. She had always seemed grateful for everything he had done. Was it all a cover?

“I need your answer quickly. We must hurry if you are coming with me. I can sense a change in the atmosphere, and I refuse to be caught. I still have much to do to execute my revenge.”

Unwilling to take the chance that she was wrong, he replied, “I will go with you for now. If your instincts prove to be wrong, I can always return.”

She held out her hand, “Grab my hand, we don’t have much time.”

Once his hand was in hers, she closed her eyes and started chanting. He watched in amazement as his surroundings swirled around him. It was as if she was creating a vortex for them to travel in. The next thing he knew they were somewhere deep in the swamplands. He wasn't sure if even his lightning speed would have gotten them here any quicker.

As much as he hated the thought of starting over, his impending capture was much worse. Before leaving, he sent out a telepathic message to his children, letting them know they should flee and flee fast; their time in the carnival had come to an end. He, however, would make certain his plans came to fruition.

Chapter 32

Mike and Hutch pulled up at the carnival at the same time. They both stared at the empty spot where the carnival had once stood. Almost everything that had been here a few hours ago was gone. There were a few rides and booths left behind, but the travel trailers and vehicles were all gone.

Mike kicked at the ground, stirring up dust, "Mon Dieu, who could have tipped them off about us getting ready to move in."

Hutch closed her eyes and breathed in the air before stating, "Someone came into the ring leader's trailer this morning and warned him that we were close. As they were leaving, he warned his workers that the police were on the way, and it was time to disband. I don't get the sense that they disbanded. Most of them fled together. We should be able to find them fairly easy, but as far as those that did separate from the rest of the group, it will be harder to find them. I'm sorry Mike. I wish I could help you, but we just don't have a lot to go on."

Mike said gruffly, "Let's walk around and see if we can find anything that will give us some clues."

As they walked around the grounds, a shiver went down Hutch's spine. There in the middle of the carnival was the fun house; the very thing she had been having nightmares about.

Mike sensed a change in her as she walked towards it. "Is there something wrong?"

She let out a small laugh, "I have been having nightmares about this place, more specifically the fun house, since I came here the other night. It brought back childhood memories that I would rather not remember."

He took her hand in his, "Would you like me to walk in there with you? Maybe, it would help ease your fears."

She shook her head, "I don't know if I can go in there. If I tell you what I am really thinking, you will think I am crazy."

He let out a laugh, "Maybe not. I have my own suspicions about what has been going on here and when I mentioned it to my partner, he thought I was nuts."

She let out a deep sigh before continuing, "Ever since I was little, I have had a unique gift. When I walk into a crime scene, I can take myself back In time to see exactly what happened. My grandmother told me that I could read the energy left behind. She taught me how to embrace my gift instead of hiding from it."

He turned her to him, "I don't think that is strange. I think a lot of cops have that capability, they just don't realize they have it."

She looked up at him, "But that isn't all that made me uneasy about this case. When I was surveying the first crime scene, the killer found out that I could read it. He intruded on my thoughts." She looked up at him with fear in her eyes, "I have never had that happen before."

He took both of her hands in his and squeezed. "The informant that was murdered told me some things that I am not sure you would believe."

"What, that we are dealing with something other than a human? I have been sensing that. The puncture wounds on the neck and the mind reading have me considering the possibility that something supernatural is involved."

He nodded in agreement, "After working on the last case, I have learned that there is more to this earth than just what we can see and hear with our own two eyes. I still find it hard to believe that there are possibly vampires that walk this earth and yet that might be exactly what we are dealing with."

She smiled warily at him, "I think the same thing. What scares me is that these creatures were able to escape."

"Right now, we can only hope that the state troopers find the traveling carnival and capture them without any more loss of life."

No sooner than he uttered the words, his phone rang, and he saw it was Guy calling. "Please tell me you have something to go on."

"I have found some helpful information. From what I have learned, vampires do NOT like silver, crucifixes, and holy water."

As soon as Mike hung up with Guy, he told Hutch, "I need the phone number for the state trooper's office that is looking for the traveling carnival. I have found out how they may be able to protect themselves."

As soon as Hutch gave him the number, he called the captain and explained, "This will sound really strange, but I beg you to have your men implement this to keep them safe. If it turns out that I am crazy, I will take the hit, but if it keeps your men alive, then I have done my job. You are looking for a traveling carnival that we believe is run by vampires."

He grimaced when the man laughed on the other end, "I needed a laugh today. Man you let that last case get to you."

He let out an exasperated sigh, "Please, just do this for me. I'm begging you. Make sure that all of your men have crucifixes on them. Guy is getting everything that you will need to kill the vampires and even found someone who can make silver bullets. Just let me or Detective Hutcherson know if you find the traveling carnival. We will meet you there as soon as possible so that we can help you take down these criminals."

The Captain exclaimed, "I am sure you believe that you can help us capture these people, but we can handle these low lives; besides, the helicopters have located them. We have a swat team getting ready to move in."

Dread moved into Mike's gut, "Please, I implore you to do as I suggest. If we are dealing with the supernatural, regular bullets and bulletproof vests will not protect your officers' lives. What can it hurt to have them wear crucifixes? I am sure Guy will be ready in no time with everything we need."

The Captain laughed, "I am more than certain that we have enough firepower to stop these guys. You have nothing to worry about. We deal with apprehending criminals all the time."

After hanging up, Mike looked at Hutch, "I don't think they took my advice to heart. Right now, all I can do is pray that they apprehend these guys without too much trouble."

Hutch looked at him, "Well, at least it is daylight. Maybe, when they drag these vampires out into the sunlight, they will burst into flames, or something."

He leaned down and kissed Hutch right on the lips, "You, my dear, are brilliant."

Mike picked up his phone and called the Captain back, "This is Mike Bailey again. If you don't want to listen to my advice, I beg that you keep the criminals in the sunlight."

As Mike hung up the phone, he suddenly remembered what Ashley told him about sunlight and vampires. He doubted any of them had a chance to grab gallons of sunblock before fleeing. Until Guy could get there with all the necessities to stop these bloodsucking creatures, at least there was a chance that the traveling carnival could be stopped in the middle of open road where there was no where to run and hide.

He turned back to Hutch, "Now, while we wait to hear from the state troopers, what say you and I go check out this fun house?"

Hutch looked at him and then the fun house; she was unsure if she had the courage to go in there, "I don't know."

"I will be right there with you. Besides, there may be someone in there needing help, or one of the carnies could be hiding in there."

As she drew her gun, "Alright, but if I see anyone coming at me, I'm going to shoot first and ask questions later."

Mike drew his gun as well, "Sounds like a plan to me."

***

As they walked through the fun house, Hutch found herself drawn to the mirrors. She just stared at her distorted image while inspecting the mirrors. She couldn't explain it, but she swore something or someone was trying to reach out to her. She closed her eyes, hoping to read something, anything, from this attraction. Suddenly, her mind was overpowered by tormented souls. She sensed Mike walk up behind her, but she just raised her hand to keep him silent. As soon as she opened her eyes and peered back into the mirror, she understood what she had been trying to read.

All around her was pain and sorrow. It felt as if her mind was being intruded from all sides, squeezing the air from her lungs. Their pain and agony gripped at her heart. The flood of emotions ripping through her body was uncontrollable.

These poor tortured souls were confused and lost; they were trapped in a place that they couldn't escape. They had no idea that their body no longer existed. She wanted to cry out and join in their gut wrenching agony. She must find a way to free them.

A mind-numbing anger burned deep inside of her for the monster, or monsters, who did this.

She fell into his embrace. There was so much grief and despair trapped in this place. Hutch focused on the way his skin felt against hers. His heart beating against her body helped to calm her. She had never felt anything as intense as what she felt while staring at the mirror.

"I have never felt anything like this before. It was awful. I have seen death before, but nothing has broken through my senses like this. Mike, we have to help them. The souls of those who were murdered here are trapped behind the mirrors."

He looked at her puzzled, "I'm sorry. I don't think I heard you right."

She looked in the mirror and could see everything. Trapped behind the mirrors were hundreds, if not thousands, of faces writhing and stretching as they tried to free themselves from their prison. She told Mike, "These souls are in terrible agony. I don't know how to release them."

As a hand reached out from the mirror, he jumped back and asked her, "Did you see that?"

She informed him, "I honestly think they are trying to reach out to us, hoping that we can free them."

"So, do you have any idea how we should set these souls free?"

Hutch shook her head. She closed her eyes once more in an attempt to figure out how to free them. As she walked around, she felt as if she was transported back in time.

The man haunting her dreams appeared before her, except the scenery around her was very different. He was surrounded by glass jars as he stood in front of a covered black wagon. He had his hands linked together as he walked back and forth at the rear of the wagon. He had thick sideburns and even thicker, almost shoulder length hair.

He was calling out to the bystanders, "Step right up folks. We've got it all! Come see the Freak Show! Nothing like it anywhere around!" The crowd moved forward eagerly as he continued, "Come right in and forget your worries. Sit a spell and let us entertain you. There are marvels in here like you have never laid your eyes on before!"

Something about the jars caught her attention, but as she tried to move in closer for a better look, her vision shifted back to the present. She looked up at Mike and exclaimed, "He has done this for almost a century now. I think he used to capture souls and held them in glass jars. I just don't know why."

Mike informed her, "The young girl that was murdered told me that she believed he figured out a way to become more powerful by collecting the souls of those he killed. She said the souls powered the rides, but she also believed they gave him his extreme power."

A chill suddenly swept through her, "Mike, this killer is not only devoid of a soul, but he has no pity for those he killed. There is not a drop of goodness in him. Something tells me that he has always been this way."

As they tried to figure out how to free the souls, Mike's cell phone rang. Guy said, "You should hear a chopper above you at any moment. We will land where you are and head to a stretch of interstate right past Alexandria. We got them Mike. The state trooper's office was ordered to listen to us."

As soon as Guy hung up, Mike pulled Hutch towards the chopper, "Let's go. I'll explain on the way up."

Once they were settled, Guy gave them each a crucifix to wear. "They haven't pulled over the caravan just yet. They have been following them at a safe distance and from what they can tell the undercover car hasn't been discovered. I found some pure silver bullets; each of the bullets has been made with special care. Inside is a tiny liquid capsule filled with a combination of Holy Water, garlic juice, and a special ultraviolet mixture that will spread into the vampire quickly upon impact. I told the state troopers that if the caravan did notice them and started to run under no circumstances should they let them go. Believe it or not, I have found a few ideas on ways to kill the vampires. One is by lighting them on fire. I told the dispatcher to inform the patrol cars if need be light the caravan on fire and let it go. If nothing else, we will have a bunch of charred carnies."

Hutch looked at the two of them, "Do you both really believe that we may be dealing with real vampires?"

Mike replied, "Yes, I do. I talked to one, and if she was faking it, then she was really good at it. I do realize that she could have had her teeth altered, but I believed her. As I said, the last case I worked as a police detective opened my eyes to the paranormal. There is more on this earth than just us."

Hutch knew what her mind was telling her, but she was not sure she was ready to grasp the possibilities that there could be real live vampires walking this earth. However, she guessed she better be ready to believe before they got there. They were getting ready to walk into the big unknown, and that was something she didn't like.

As the caravan neared the road block, Hutch's fingers drummed against her gun holster. The interstate was devoid of any life except for them. No one wanted any of the general public to be killed, so they shut down the road. They landed a few seconds ago and the dust had yet to settle. Her heart raced when she saw the caravan as it neared. This was it; the moment they had been waiting for. The lead vehicle was the first one to see the road block. Even though technically there was no food being cooked in the procession, she swore she could smell the scent of hot dogs and popcorn from here.

She watched as the caravan slammed on its brakes; the screech pierced the air. The engines began to shut off one by one; however, no one attempted to exit the vehicles. A mixture of anticipation and fear built up inside of her body. She despised this waiting game; she was ready for one of them to make a move.

A movement coming from the cab of the head vehicle caught everyone's attention. Instead of stepping out as instructed, he fired his gun right through the windshield. They took him down in no time. His death wasn't as spectacular as what Hutch had envisioned. She pictured that he would combust into a shower of dust, but instead, he just dropped right where he had been shot.

They took cover as the others came out with guns drawn. It wasn't until a movement from the rear trailer that showed them exactly what they were dealing with. The man, or creature to be more exact, moved quicker than any of them had expected. He grabbed an officer and tossed him high into the air as if he was a piece of trash. A fellow officer shot him before he could progress to anyone else. They watched in amazement as the man burst into a shower of dust. Realizing that they were dealing with something beyond their realm of expertise, they waited to see what would exit from the vehicles next.

Mike whispered to Hutch, "Can you try to sense if there are any hostages?"

Hutch closed her eyes and attempted to hear if anyone was calling out for her help. She could feel their presence, but she was uncertain if they were alive or trapped in the contraptions. "I can't say Mike. It is hard to tell if they are alive and being held hostage or if their souls are trapped."

He nodded in understanding. Since they were unsure about any potential hostages, they couldn't risk blowing everything up.

Mike instructed those moving in, "Remember, we have no idea what we are dealing with as we go in. Shoot first and ask questions later. That may be the only way to save your life."

As the officers moved in on the trailers, they fingered their crucifixes, now believing in the supernatural.

***

It had been a long, hard day by the time it was over. Mike had no idea how many they killed or how many got away before they found the caravan. He did know that they somehow left behind no survivors and lost four state troopers in the process.

Hutch mentioned that she had a very strong feeling the ringleader of the carnival escaped. She still sensed his presence.

The whole carnival was being brought to the state trooper's impound yard where they would gather as much evidence as they could. They would attempt to figure out who lived in the trailers by using DNA.   It would be a long, tedious process. Guy was also searching for someone who could help release the souls trapped in the mirrors.

Mike hoped someone out there could help them. As he was walking around the rides one more time, he found Hutch staring at the carousel. She looked up at him, "I won't ever look at a carnival the same way again."

He nodded his head in agreement, "Come on. There is nothing else we can do here."

As they walked away from the carnival, she grabbed his hand and placed her head on his shoulder. He brought her closer to him. The one good thing that came out of this case was that he might have found someone he could spend the rest of his life with.

Thank you!

Dear Reader,

Thank you for purchasing this book. I hope you enjoyed reading this novel as much as I enjoyed writing it.

It is very important for me to hear what you think about the book.   Your reviews give me inspiration in my future writings. You can leave a review on Amazon, Goodreads or Barnes and Noble.

Your thoughts and opinions mean a lot to me.

Please enjoy a sample of Redemption. Josie is determined to find the vampire who turned her a century ago. What she didn't expect to find was a blood trafficking ring. Can she stop this injustice or does the corruption run deeper than she feared?

Also, be sure to check out my website and social media sites for upcoming books and giveaways.

Sincerely,

Mary Theriot

Links

Website www.maryreasontheriot.com

Goodreads for reviews -
http://www.goodreads.com/MaryReasonTheriot

Facebook - http://goo.gl/Sd0VgY

Twitter - @Mktheriot

Google+ - +MaryTheriot

YouTube - http://goo.gl/ErM1M6

Pinterest - http://www.pinterest.com/mktheriot

Blog Page - www.maryreasontheriot.me

Redemption

Where Darkness Reigns

Book 4

Josie's Story

By: Mary Reason Theriot

Chapter 1

The master vampire looked over at his mistress, "Did you have success this time, mon cher?"

Ezrielle observed the man who had become her most recent lover, "Soon, cher, soon. This little experiment of mine was not as successful as I hoped."

Ezrielle snapped her fingers as a creature walked from the shadows. "I will call this one Grunch."

He looked over the creature and was taken aback by its grotesque features, "It is but a goat in the body of a man."

"Ah, but this particular Grunch is unique. At one time, he was a vampire. This creature craves human blood."

Pulling her into his arms, he whispered, "I am beginning to lose faith in your abilities, mon cher. This creature you created took no imagination at all, my dear."

Furious, Ezrielle pushed him away, "You dare question my powers!" Tsking him, "That is not wise."

His eyes turned red as his true form took shape. She could see the outline of the evil lurking beneath him, daring to break free from its human constraints, "It is not wise to threaten me. The Dukes of Hell may have granted you immortality, but with one bite, I can send you back to your maker."

Ezrielle attempted to placate him, "These are nothing but simple experiments." She called out to one of her Rougarou, "I still have other creatures that I am working on.

My Rougarou is more than enough to protect your children.”

The master nodded in approval, “My Joshua needs some for his own purposes. I will pay handsomely for his and mine as well.”

“As you wish. Come tonight and claim your Rougarou. I will make sure that the packs for each of you will obey your commands.”

The master looked over at the creatures Ezrielle had created in disgust, “You know, mon cher, I do believe the civilized world would frown upon what you do here.”

“Ah, but, the civilized world will have a hard time finding me. The only way you can find me is if I allow it. If I truly wanted to, I could keep you from finding me as well.”

Chapter 2

Tyler immediately spotted the woman across the street. Her beauty held him mesmerized. She beguiled him with her bewitching eyes and long flowing hair twisting in the wind. She was the fairest maiden he had ever seen.

When she beckoned him to her, he went willingly. The distance between them closed fast; her beauty pulled him to her. He dared not utter a word as she slipped her hand in his. She looked up at him with such sweet innocence; it took his breath away.

Unable to stop himself, his mouth seized hers in a kiss that rocked him to the core. Her deep, ruby red lips were succulent, beyond anything he'd ever known. He tasted their sweetness and it made him crave even more. His heart pounded ferociously in his chest.

He entwined his fingers in her hair to bring her closer to him. She smiled up at him as the energy around them turned frenetic. Urgency began to fill him. Being young and inexperienced with women, he was clumsy and unsure how to handle himself in the presence of such a beautiful woman.

He was drawn to her, wanting to grant her every wish. She pulled him along behind her, leading him away like a puppy dog deep into the swamps and away from the town.

As her long cloak flowed in the wind, he saw a glimpse of her body. His breath caught at the mere sight of a bare ankle.

As they entered a clearing in the swamp, she pulled him into her arms. He moaned in sheer ecstasy as her body pressed against his. He had never met a woman as brazen as she. Kissing him fervently, she took everything he had to give. Desire took over all conscious thought.

Without warning, her passionate kisses turned cold. Torches broke the tree line and bathed them both in the flickering light. Chants filled the air around him. He looked at her beseechingly, unsure of what was happening.

Ezrielle ran her finger along his strong jaw line, "I was ruined by a man much like you once, mon cher. He soon learned the cost of betraying me." Kissing him once more, she continued, "I decided then and there to teach all men a lesson. No longer will they use women, ruin their lives and toss them aside like an old tattered rag."

The homunculi, evil little creatures created by an alchemist, began to form a tight circle around them. The creatures were barely four feet tall and all bone, muscle and sinew. Pure terror paralyzed Tyler.

From the darkness, a vile creature, standing just over five feet tall and covered with fine hair, appeared. It had cloven hooves for feet and the short tail of a goat. Even the head of the creature resembled a goat more than a man, complete with a small pair of horns protruding from the top of its head. A large pair of red eyes glowed in the dark as it moved closer to Tyler. He bit back a scream as the vile creature opened its mouth, full of long, sharp fangs dripping with blood, to let out an ear piercing scream.

Ezrielle greeted the creature, "Welcome my pet." She turned to Tyler, "This is one of my latest creations. It is a

Grunch, half-man and half-goat. He and a few of his brothers protect the perimeters of my land." She ran a finger along his strong jaw line, "But you, mon cher, will be something so much more." From the darkness, even more creatures arrived. These creatures had the shape of half-wolf and half-man. With a sinister smile, Ezrielle taunted Tyler, "These are my Rougarou. They will be your brothers." She looked over at the Rougarou forming a circle around them. "Welcome your new brother, my loves."

Sensing the young man's discomfort, the voodoo priestess ran her hands over his well-defined body, "You have the Dukes of Hell and alchemists to thank for my powers and pets." As she stretched languidly in the moonlight, "The Dukes of Hell gave me what I desired most you see – immortality." Taking one of the ravens out from the cage, Ezrielle cut open its chest, and removed its still beating heart with a long nail. She ran the bloody muscle along Tyler's lips as he tried to avoid the ghastly thing, "For you see, when a woman stays young and beautiful forever; the world will be hers."

Tyler watched in horror as she swallowed the beating heart in one gulp. Once more, he tried to free himself, unsure how he'd landed in this nightmare. As the torches were extinguished and the darkness enveloped the area, he felt the icy grasp of death near him. Looking up to the full moon, he questioned what he did to deserve this.

He turned his gaze to the woman. This time, he didn't see her for the beautiful woman she portrayed, but instead, the woman she truly was. His eyes were no longer clouded with desire and infatuation. She purposefully lured him here to his own demise.

As the chanting continued, a piercing cold spread throughout him that turned him from a human to that of a Rougarou. Before long, the cold turned into a burning fire. The blood inside of his veins felt as if it were literally boiling. As the chanting increased, rising in tempo, his skin began to melt off and was replaced with fur. He screamed out in agony as his body was transformed into the hideous Rougarou.

Available in eBook and Paperback

You can also follow Joshua and Bianca's story in "Seduced by Voodoo". The battle of good versus evil will soon take place in the bayous of New Orleans, Louisiana. Bianca Honore with her new vampire lover, Joshua, will raise an army of the living dead. Can Father Mark Trahan stop this ever growing evil before it is too late?